ONCE MORE ON THE EDGE

a Christian novel by Carrie E. Robinson

The sequel to The Plan, The Thought, The Purpose

© 2016 by Carrie E. Robinson

Published by Carrie E. Robinson

Printed in the United States of America by Createspace

All rights Reserved

Library of Congress Cataloging-in-Publication Data

Once More On The Edge – April 11, 2016

ISBN-13:978-0692659663 (Carrie E. Robinson)

ISBN-10:0692659668

ONCE MORE ON THE EDGE

A CHRISTIAN NOVEL BY CARRIE E ROBINSON

A SEQUEL TO THE PLAN THE THOUGHT THE PURPOSE

When God leads you to the edge of the cliff, trust Him fully and let go. Only one of two things will happen: either He'll catch you when you fall, or He'll teach you how to fly!

Author unknown

To Lonnie
My great nephew
Let Go and Let God –
He Got You !! Love you
Aunt Carrie Robinson

CELEBRATING THE LOVING MEMORIES

OF

MY GRANDMOTHER DAISY J. HERRING-WALKER

MY FATHER JIMMY DUNHAM

MY MOTHER MARY L. DUNHAM

MY BROTHER ARTIS C. DUNHAM

MY SISTER MARY E. DUNHAM-BUIE

MY SISTER DOROTHY E. DUNHAM-DARRISON

MY NEPHEW CHARLES L. DUNHAM, SR

MY NEPHEW ANTWAN DUNHAM

DEACON HENRY RAWLS

FIREMAN RONNIE L. HENDERSON 9/11/2001

MY FATHER-IN-LAW MERRILL E. ROBINSON, SR

MY MOTHER-IN-LAW IDA MAE PERRY-ROBINSON

*MY SISTER-IN-LAW MARILYN "PUDDY"
ROBINSON*

MY SISTER-IN-LAW RENEE "BO-PEEP" ROBINSON

MY SISTER-IN-LAW JUANITA HAYES-DUNHAM

MY BROTHER-IN-LAW ROBERT J.WINFIELD, JR.

MY BROTHER-IN-LAW LEROY DARRISON

MY NIECE SHARON THORNTON-MORROW

MY FRIEND IRENE MOTES

WHAT PEOPLE ARE SAYING ABOUT

THE PLAN, THE THOUGHT, THE PURPOSE

THE SEQUEL TO ONCE MORE ON THE EDGE.

By Dr. Tina Whitfield, DHA of Clayton, NC

I enjoyed every minute of this book. I could not, and did not, put it down until I was finished. Mrs. Robinson captivated me with suspense, love, faith, hope, and praise. She depicted the very essence of how individuals can often forget God in our daily lives. The book is so intriguing that I will continue to recommend her book to everyone. I can hardly wait to read her next book.

By Gerilynne Lampkin, of Avon Park, Fl

Wow! If I could rate this book 10 stars I would definitely without a doubt award it 10 stars. The book grabs the reader's attention from the first page to the last page. I read this book in one day. I was not able to put the book down. The characters in this book come to life. I am amazed at the creative writing of Carrie Robinson. This book will become a movie (Gods timing). If you are looking for a book that encourages readers to take a look at their own lives this is the book to read. I highly recommend this book to all women. You do not have to have a PhD behind your name to become captivated throughout the book. I think all women regardless of race, creed, and economical status should read this book. After, you read the book take a look in the mirror and see what God reveals to you.

By <u>Deborah Beckwith</u> of First Baptist Church Manna.,Va.

This novel is fantastic. This book has blessed my soul in so many ways. I laughed and I cried I felt sorry for certain characters. I felt the presence of God to the point where I threw up my hands and praise the Lord right along with the person's involved. It held my attention. And I was always thinking I gotta get back and read the next chapter. I felt like I was actually there. I recommend this novel to all my friends and family. For the year of 2015 I plan to apply some of what I have learn and read in this book to my life.

By <u>Joshua Forkiner,</u> of Phoenix, Arizona

This book was definitely a page turner and brilliantly refreshing! The book took you threw many emotions from laughing to tears in a matter of pages! Demonstrating different perspectives on life and what triggered Faith in each character as they went thru trials and tribulations in everyday life. The book was filled with inspiration, truth and empowerment to tackle all of life obstacles. If you have not read this book do yourself a favor and get a copy truly a MUST READ!!!!!!!!!!!!

By <u>Dr. Nelson McAllister</u>, M,TH.DD of Calvary Full Gospel Family Church Center of Newburgh, NY

Intriguing and thought provoking! It causes one to think about their own life and how it intertwines with those we love and associate with.

By <u>Catherine Roundtree-Cliff</u>, BME, Entrepreneur of Rochester, NY

I enjoyed reading this book. It kept my attention and I could not put it down until I read it in its entirety. Carrie did an amazing job in bring life to the story!

By Rev. Blessie Vandervort, B.TH, M.TH

A real page turner, this book grabbed me from the first page and kept me turning pages to the end. I loved how Ms. Robinson used the genre of fiction then filled it with Biblical truth, inspiration, and encouragement. Just the kind of book I as a Christian look for: romance without vulgarity, true love that has stood the test of time, and how the love of a good person can cause someone not so good to want to be better. All through this book Ms Robinson kept the reader's focus on God and His undying love for His children. I really enjoyed this book. Congratulations and thanks, Ms Carrie Robinson for a wonderful read.

By Octavia Royal, Health Care Specialist,

This book is a page turner. You will laugh and cry from the beginning to end. This is truly a must read. I can't wait for the sequel.

By Weldon & Patricia Dunham, Veteran Admin of Ga.

Awesome! What an inspiring book! Very captivating and articulately written, page after page after page. I love it. May blessings be upon you for delivering such a profound exposure of life and how awesome our God is.

By Daisy Winfield-Ponder, RN of Newburgh, NY

This was such a great read! Definitely a page turner. I just couldn't wait to see what happened next. Every part of a persons' emotions were displayed in this book and so many decisions we make in life were also present. When is the sequel coming?

By Bobby and Diane Dunham, RN of Evans, Ga.

Carrie! what a dynamic and uplifting book! As soon as people realize that God and only the Almighty Father is in control, we can live a fulfilled Christian life. Waiting for the next book.

DEDICATION

To My Lord and Saviour Jesus Christ, the Son of the Living God and to the Power of His Spirit. Thank you for the gift to write and share your ways in the style in which you have given me. All glory and honor belongs to you.

To my husband, Merrill E. Robinson, Jr.

You continue to reveal to me my inner strength daily as I have cared endlessly for you the past 8 years. You are an amazing man with supernatural stamina to live life to its fullest! To death do we part, my endless love.

To my children, Juella Guadalupe, Peppur Robinson, and Jodis Robinson

You all continue to teach me the importance of prayer and how powerful it really is. I am so grateful for the many lessons you all have taught me as a mother.

To all of my Face Book Readers, Family and Friends

If it had not been for your encouraging words impregnating my mind to pen this book as a sequel, it would have not been birthed. Thanks for believing in me.

To My Good Friend, Maggie O. McAllister

For your diligence and the many sacrifices you made in helping me to edit this novel and encouraging me to pen the sequel… Well, here it is my friend!!

FOREWORD

Here's a book that captures your attention to the point you forget all appointments and burn your food while you are cooking! It's so captivating you will forget what you are doing at the moment. To maximize the fullness of this sequel, you must read the authors' first book, The Plan, The Thought, The Purpose. It is filled with spiritual humor, factual intrigue and suspense. Carrie Robinson is an extraordinary author who has a God given ability to pen in a way that foster self evaluation and thought provoking illustrations that presents another perception of truth.

Apostle Clara Lawrence of Raleigh, NC
Daughters of Zion United International

When I say you will have great difficulty putting this book down once you start reading it, I really mean just that!! During the adventure of reading this book you will find yourself riveted until the last words fill your taste buds, leaving you drooling for more. It is a page turner full of real life lessons and it will definitely evoke a myriad of emotions – anger-joy-resolve and thanksgiving.

Jacqueline (Dunham) Gregory,
Administrative Assistant ~ U.S. Coast Guard HQ

FOREWORD CONTINUED

Evangelist Robinson has created an outstanding gospel adventure with detailed outlines of the power and transformation of the Holy Spirit in ones' life. Momma King efficacious faith and prayer opens the pathway to forgiveness, reconciliation, miracles and healing. The author's ability to convey the power of God's miracles in the adventure is especially enticing; as well as the unadulterated truth. It is amazing! I look forward to reading more.

Rev. Jerry Dunham MA Psychology
Chiplona, Spain

I am most intrigued by the Author, Carrie Robinson and her ingenious God-given gift to weave scriptures into the plot of each episode in this book. It will make an indelible mark on each reader, saved or unsaved, atheist or believer. It is truly God's anointing that dwells within Carrie to be able to uniquely intertwine God's Word in such a way that you can see God's hand at work in the lives of some of the characters and the devil working in others. This book is very meaningful, and enlightening of good and evil at work, and the end results either being blessed or cursed, depending on which master you choose to obey. While keeping it real, Carrie made this reading interesting, fun, and more importantly life changing.

Evangelist Veronica Rawls
of Timberlake, NC

A NOTE FROM CARRIE

To introduce this book is to walk down memory lane in perhaps your life, my life or perhaps someone you know or once knew; it is with my God given talents, vivid imagination and a bit of humor that I share these life lessons in a tangible, authentic but realistic way. I am a firm believer that we are bound to face many obstacles and challenges in life, but how you handle each situation conveys your level of faith in God or faith in your own abilities. If we settle within ourselves that God loves us and desires good things for us, then when the bad things happens, we find comfort in knowing there is something good that will come from it. Therefore we have faith in God and trust Him that He always knows what's best for us. Everything that happens pushes us further along into our divine destiny, fulfilling God's purpose and plan for our lives...good, bad or indifferent. Sometimes life lessons can be unbearable and painful, but there is a level of comfort, trust and confidence that supersedes everything in knowing God is with us and all things seen and unseen are working together for our good.

Often times we petition God for a certain thing and when it doesn't come in the nicely wrapped package we think it should be, we reject it, not understanding it is just the outer wrapping, but the best is on the inside. We tend to trust what is tangible and what we see on the surface, but real trust in God is having blind faith and confidence that He knows exactly what is best for us and we accepts what He has for us without kicking and screaming.

Recently, God told me He was "trimming the fat" from around me. (Physically would have been nice, but I knew He was speaking spiritually☺). I did not want to let go of what had become familiar to me. Many times we try to hold on to the things that are no longer needed or useful to us. It is those times, we tend to trust in our own abilities and find ourselves **once more on the edge**; but, when we learn to let go we make room for the greater blessings that God has for us. What are you still holding on to? Let Go and Let God.

ONCE MORE ON THE EDGE

CHAPTER 1

Teresa was emotionally devastated and drained from her close encounter of being incarcerated and charged with drug trafficking. Although the charges were unfounded and she was released, her boyfriend, Ricky Clay, was found guilty and sentenced to 15 years to life. She was extremely grateful that God granted her unmerited favor, but still in denial of Ricky's heinous deeds done to her and her son. She was hopelessly in love with a shrewd criminal who used her for his own interests. For the past six months her routine was the same: work, picking up Jamie from Momma King and back home; no social life, no romance, no Ricky. She cried herself to sleep nearly every night; but continued to put on a happy face for Jamie, her nine year old son and Momma King, her long-time friend and confidante. She was deeply depressed and had a hard time concentrating on the smallest tasks, especially on her job.

Troy Kennedy, Teresa's attorney, continued to call her even after the court hearing was over; she however, would not return his calls. She knew he was deeply disappointed because she refused to press charges against Ricky for kidnapping her and Jamie and leaving them in an old abandoned shack. She somehow convinced herself that Jamie's version of what happened that night was right. Which was: Ricky took them to the old isolated, dilapidated shack to protect them from the bad guys and that he really was coming back for them, but was arrested.

The real truth was Ricky's BOYS (Dante, Billy, minus Henry and Big Red, who was killed in a robbery), had just arrived from out of state to celebrate and collect on their biggest pay-out ever...3.5 million dollars. Ricky thought Teresa had stolen the money from him and when she denied taking the money; he knocked her out with a punch to the head, tied her hands and drove her and Jamie to the old shack on the outskirts of town. He was in conflict as to whether or not Teresa actually took the money, but she seemed to be the only suspect that could have taken it. Uncertain about what to do, he thought leaving them in the old shack would be frightening enough that Teresa would confess that she had taken the money and reveal where she had hidden it. With no confession and no money, he had no other choice but to leave them there while he went to break the devastating news to his BOYS that somehow the money had disappeared. He feared his BOYS would believe he had double crossed them and took the money for himself and possibly retaliate against Teresa and Jamie. He did care about Teresa and Jamie. The BOYS were like his brothers, and he knew they could be coldblooded and dangerous if they felt they had been betrayed. He was planning to go back and get Jamie and Teresa after talking to the BOYS (if he lived), but was arrested shortly after leaving them in the shack.

Ricky did not know that Nate Bishop, the owner of Paradise Pillows, had stumbled onto the drugs he was smuggling through his warehouse. Unsure as to what to do, Nate summoned the Feds to stake out his company. While under surveillance they observed Ricky and his contact, Big Mc, unloading the drugs into Big Mc's van and they witnessed the pay off money being loaded into the trunk of Ricky's car. Later, when Ricky went inside the office, the Feds created a small diversion by sending an agent inside to place a bogus order of pillows to occupy Ricky, while another Federal Agent picked the lock of the trunk and seized the money. Ricky later discovered the money missing when he went to the bank to put it into a safe deposit box.

Troy on the other hand had tried his best to persuade Teresa that Ricky had committed an atrocious act, a felony by taking her against her will, not to mention endangering the welfare of Jamie. No matter what he said, Teresa was not budging and would not allow herself to think anything negative about Ricky. As her attorney, he tried to respect her decision. He knew she was emotionally distraught from yet another painful broken relationship; but it had been six months. He wanted her to know he was there for her, but he also did not want to be too pushy. He called at least once a week just to say hi and would leave a message for her expressing his concern, and asked her to please give him a call back. She never did.

Feeling hopeless, he decided to call Momma King to inquire about Teresa. She informed him that she was still healing and doing a lot of pretending, but still hurting and fighting depression. She seems almost natural when interacting with Jamie, but otherwise very much a recluse. Jamie keeps asking her where is Ricky. She seems lost for words and it is obvious to me that she did not tell Jamie that Ricky is incarcerated. Let's keep on praying for her, okay?"

"Sure thing," Troy replied, surprised that Teresa had not told Jamie about Ricky yet. "Perhaps I can help her with that," he offered. "You know, she has to go to court to see Judge Harris tomorrow to get her records expunged; I plan to be there just in case she needs me. I guess she wants to try to handle it all on her own now, but it has been six months and to be quite frank Ms. King, I would love to see her again. She is a very beautiful woman."

Surprised by his comment, Ms. King, exclaimed, "Well, Glory to God! God slipped this one in on me, smiling at the thought of him and Teresa as a couple. Well, you go on and meet her tomorrow. I think it's just what she needs."

Teresa was still hurting badly, and everything at work reminded her of Ricky as much as she loved Nate and his company, Paradise Pillows, it seemed very hard to stay focused and do her job. Ricky had worked hard building the business for Nate the past four years. Nate hired him as the maintenance technician, but Ricky had other calculated ideas. He quickly began to show Nate how to triple his business and build a stronger clientele. Nate loved him as his own son, and trusted him wholeheartedly. Ricky and Teresa had been inseparable from the first day Nate hired him.

Teresa had worked for Nate for over a decade and there were just too many reminders of her now shattered life. She decided she and Jamie would take a little vacation after her six-month probation was over. Even thinking of that was difficult because she, Ricky and Jamie always vacationed together, and now this was another painful reminder. It was hard to escape Ricky's presence. He was still everywhere and in everything she attempted to do. Just looking at Jamie missing Ricky and not understanding why he was suddenly no longer in his life was devastating enough; now he was acting out in school. His grades dropped and she had to go to his school twice in the past three weeks to meet with the psychologist because Jamie was fighting and bullying his classmates.

"Spring break is next week and perhaps I can get him back on track by taking him on a little vacation. It will be good for the both of us," she thought.

Teresa often reflected back to the day in court when she attacked Ricky and called him names and was physically removed from the courtroom. Even though he did her wrong and hurt her, she still loved him. It was painful watching Jamie become more confused as to why Ricky was not coming around anymore. Not knowing what to tell him, she told him Ricky had a family emergency in Chicago and had to go back home to his family for a while.

"But why doesn't he call you or me Momma," he inquired, "do you think the bad guys that were coming for us got him?"

"Oh no, I think he is okay. I don't have a number to call so we will just have to wait to hear from him. Now don't you worry about Ricky and the bad guys, you hear me?"

"Yes ma'am, but I miss him so much Momma."

"I know baby, me too," giving him a hug and a kiss on his forehead. "Now, you go on and get ready for bed. There's school tomorrow and please promise me no more fighting okay?"

"Yes Ma'am."

"I love you Jamie Hayward."

"I know Momma, I love you too. Good night," as he headed off to bed.

"I will be there shortly to tuck you in bed," Teresa yelled.

Teresa felt so guilty at times because she had almost six months of letters stored in her safe from Ricky. She could not believe she still loved him and could not bring herself to tell Jamie or Momma King that she had received so many letters from him. She was embarrassed that she was so weak and vulnerable. What would Momma King, Nate Bishop or Troy Kennedy really think of her? She tried to convince herself that she was not attached to Ricky anymore. She would take the letters from the mailbox and hold them to her heart, but would not allow herself to read them. It was her safety net to keep him at bay so she thought. She felt if she did not read whatever he had to say, it would be easier to get over him and move on with her life; but, the truth of the matter was evident. She was still stuck, naive, and vulnerable and in love with a criminal, who had received a 15-year to life sentence. She could no longer hold back the tears that rolled down her cheeks. Ricky Clay still held her captive, even from prison.

"Momma, are you coming to tuck me in?" Jamie yelled from his bedroom.

"Uh yes, sweetie, I am coming right now," as she wiped the tears from her eyes.

After tucking Jamie in bed, Teresa went back to her bedroom and opened the safe. She picked up the shoe box that held Ricky's letters and slowly and carefully opened the box as if it was the most precious possession she had ever owned.

"Oh, Ricky, I can't bear to read your letters yet. It is still so painful and I love you so much even though you don't deserve my love. I can't just turn my emotions off. I am trying to survive and keep my sanity right now. I hope you understand why I can't read your letters now. Why did you have to mess things up for us. We were a perfect family and Jamie adores you. Why Ricky, why?" she cried, clutching a handful of the unopened letters to her heart. In her disparaging cry, she drifted off to sleep. It was three thirty that morning when she woke up, disorientated and confused. It seemed as if Ricky was there with her and asked her for forgiveness. She remembered saying "of course Ricky, I forgive you. I love you." The hugs and kisses felt so real, and the scent of Paul Sebastian, Ricky's favorite cologne seemed to still linger in the air. Teresa began to really question her sanity.

"Oh God please help me. What is happening to me?" she cried, "I can't go on like this."

Teresa tried to fall back to sleep but to much was going on in her mind. She decided she would put Ricky's letters in order chronologically, (so that if she ever did decide to read them they would be in sync). This little project was helpful and only took a few minutes. Still not able to sleep and knowing she had to go to court to see Judge Harris in the morning, she put the letters back in the safe and took her Bible from the night stand next to her bed.

Sitting Indian style in her bed with the Bible in her lap and hands lifted towards heaven, she said, "*Okay God, I don't know where the answer is in your Word, but I know you know exactly what I need to read and what I need to know. Speak to me Father God. Please, in Jesus name.* Teresa began to sing songs and worship the Lord. She emptied her heart to God. It was almost 5AM when she randomly opened the Bible. She read the 6th chapter of Romans. Certain verses seemed to leap right from the page and into her heart. Verse 12 *"Therefore do not let sin reign in your mortal (earthly) body, that you should obey it in its lusts. 13 And do not present your members (body parts) as instruments of unrighteousness to sin, but present yourselves to God as being alive from the dead and your members (body parts) as instruments of righteousness to God. 21 What fruit did you have then in the things of which you are now ashamed? For the end of those things is death."*

"Now wait a minute God," she protested. "Am I supposed to feel ashamed for having natural sexual relations with the man I love? I loved Ricky and he loved me. Well at least I thought he loved me and Jamie, correcting herself. Wow, look at me! I am a mess! I loved Michael Harden, Jamie's father. I thought he loved me too, and he walked out on Jamie and me, when he was only 4 months old. What is wrong with me? This seems to be a pattern of some sort. Why can't I find a man that really loves me? I need clarity God. I loved them and they in return hurt me and misused me. Why do I always seem to get the losers, she questioned God. Am I not pretty enough, or smart enough to get a man willing to take me down the aisle and marry me and love me the way I am supposed to be loved? What is wrong with me?" Teresa paused and continued to read.

22 But now having been set free from sin and having become slaves of God you have your fruit to holiness and the end, everlasting life. 23 For the wages of sin is death, but the gift of God is eternal life in Christ Jesus our Lord.

Teresa suddenly had an epiphany that the intimate relationship she had with Ricky was displeasing to God. Fornication is sin. She had never given it any thought. It was natural and normal until reading these scriptures. *"Oh God please forgive me,"* she cried until she was exhausted and fell asleep clutching her Bible to her chest.

CHAPTER 2

Jamie's father, Michael Hayden abandoned him when he was four months old, nine years ago. Michael reflected back to the night. He had been with Tavia, a woman who he found comforting and not at all complicated. She had no children and did not want any. Unlike Teresa, who had just given birth to his son. It was not part of the plan to get pregnant. It just happened and Teresa refused to have an abortion as Michael suggested. Michael felt betrayed and trapped. He did not want any children and after the birth of Jamie, he began to stay out more and more with Tavia. He would meet her a few times during the week after work for a few drinks and "comforting companionship." He recalled the last night he saw Teresa and Jamie. He had come home late again as usual and had lost his key to the apartment. Teresa opened the door screaming at him. She knew there was another woman and he was given an ultimatum. It is either her or the other woman. He made the decision that night. He left.

After leaving Teresa, he and his girlfriend, Tavia, moved to Austin, Texas and lived together until their recent breakup. They just seemed to have drifted apart after he started his trucking business. He had become a very successful businessman, but sometimes he was gone for two and three weeks at a time. He would return home completely exhausted and would rest up a few days and back to work again for another two or three weeks. He made excellent money and took great pride in showering Tavia with all the monetary things she wanted, hoping it would be enough to keep her content.

It was great the first five years. Tavia was preoccupied traveling all around the world with her new friends. When they returned home to their husbands and children they actually seemed to love and miss each other. Observing the joy and happiness of her friends and their spouses when they returned to each other began to take a toll on Tavia. Michael was never there for her when she came back. She missed Michael. She would imagine that Michael was there waiting with the others to greet her with opened arms and an outward expression of love that said I missed you Tavia. She wanted more intimate time with Michael, but he was always emotionally distant or asleep when he did come home. She now wanted to have children, but he would tell her no…later, when we are more financially established. Tavia knew it was more than that because they were very established and financially secure. Tavia did not work and hated that she never had pursued her own dreams; now she felt stuck because she depended on Michael for everything. Each time she would mention starting a family, he seemed to get angry and become even more distant. It became very frustrating for Tavia to have a man and material things but no real companionship. Their relationship soon became a time of fussing and contention when he was home and awake. He had no tolerance for a nagging woman. He looked forward to getting on the road again, but this time it will be different. "I will not be coming back at least for a few months this time," he thought.

Michael stayed up most of the night, planning his next step while Tavia slept. He was very deliberate and precise and gave his life a lot of thought. He realized he did not love Tavia and it was not fair to continue on this journey to nowhere with her. He was convinced she did not love him either, just the monetary things he was able to provide for her.

The thought of Jamie and Teresa tugged more and more at Michael's heart. He wondered if Jamie looked like him. What kind of boy he turned out to be? Did he like sports or music? He was ashamed of himself and how he just left Teresa to fend for herself and his four-month-old son, Jamie. He never sent her a dime to help her. "He wondered if it was too late to be in his life. Would Teresa allow him to see Jamie, or spend any time with him at all? Well, I am going to give it my best shot. I want to make things right," he declared to himself.

The next morning Tavia woke up early. She showered and cooked Michael's favorite breakfast: country ham, scrambled eggs with green peppers and onions and creamy cheese grits and whole wheat toast with butter and marmalade jelly. The smells of his favorite foods awakened him. He grabbed his robe and joined Tavia in their breakfast nook which overlooked the lake. He kissed her on the forehead. "Ummmhh, this smells wonderful," he said salivating.

Tavia smiled nervously trying to be careful not to nag. "I am happy you are home so I can cook you a real meal. Sit down and let's eat, placing his favorite foods in front of him. Oops, I forgot your coffee," as she turned back to get his favorite coffee mug filled with hot black coffee. "I am planning on going shopping with the girls this afternoon, but I can certainly change my plans if you are not leaving right away," she said.

"Actually, I wanted to talk to you," sipping his coffee. "Do you have time?" He asked.

Tavia scowled realizing this was not the norm for Michael. He seldom held a conversation for more than five minutes before falling asleep or disengaging altogether.

"Sure Michael," she said, taking a seat opposite him.

He took a deep sigh, cleared his throat and stared down at his plate of food avoiding Tavia's eyes. He no longer had a desire for any of his favorite foods that sat before him. He slowly began, "well, I am going to take a trip to New York City and I will be gone for many months. It is a strong possibility that I will *not* be coming back. I don't want you to worry about anything for a while at least until you are able to get a job. I will be leaving you with fifty thousand dollars. The money is for you to do with as you please, but I will not be giving anymore. As you already know, this house is paid for and you can live in it or sell it. The deed has been modified with only your name on it.

27

This is your house and everything in it, car included. I am sorry this had to be this way but it is the best thing for both of us. Nine years ago when we got together in New York, I ran away with you to escape a woman who had a child for me that I did not want and I never looked back. I was a selfish cowardly man, afraid of commitment and responsibility. The other day on my way home, I heard a preacher say on the radio, "*If a man does not take care of his own he is worse than an infidel.*" Michael was not sure what an infidel was but he concluded it was not good and made a mental note to look it up when he got home.

"Since then," he continued, "my son and his mother have consumed my thoughts and I can't shake it anymore. I longed to see them. I am sorry but I must go back to check on them and try to make things right. Plus, I realize you nag me because you are not happy and I am denying you the things you want, like a family and a real husband. Now you are free to find someone who will treat you and love you the way you deserve to be loved and treated."

Tavia sat still staring directly at Michael, taking in every word as tears rolled down her cheeks. When Michael finally was able to look up, tears were rolling down his cheeks as well. Tavia got up and walked over and hugged him. They cried together. Michael said, "I am really sorry I hurt you Tavia."

"No it is good for both of us, she protested. I understand and I am not mad. I am actually happy to see you finally do something that you want to do to make things right. Not only in your life, but mine as well. You are a good man Michael and I appreciate your generosity. You will always be a good friend to me and I am here for you if you ever need to talk to someone. I feel I truly understand you and perhaps when you were younger you were selfish and inconsiderate, but I have lived with you almost nine years now and you are the most selfless and kind hearted person I have ever known. I wish you all the best Michael and I love you for having the heart to allow us both to be free. They continued to cry and hold each other for quite some time. Finally, after throwing some of his personal belonging in his customized Volvo truck, they said their goodbyes with a clean and clear conscience. Tavia stood in the driveway, waving and yelling. "Goodbye Michael. Thank you, thank you for everything," as he drove off heading for New York City.

CHAPTER 3

The sound of the alarm startled Teresa. She had a rough night and was not in the mood for anything but a few more hours of sleep and rest. Dozing back off to sleep, she was awakened again to Jamie calling. "Momma, Momma, wake up! You are going to be late for work if you don't get up and I am going to miss the bus and then you are gonna have to drive me to school, he mocked.

Teresa chuckled to herself, boy, Jamie is growing into such a big boy, but he is starting to sound just like me. He really needs a man in his life now. Again her mind drifted back to Ricky being a father figure to Jamie.

"Oh, I have to get my head on straight. Ricky is in jail and will be there for at least fifteen years, and Jamie will be a man by that time and neither one of us will need him then."

"Okay Jamie, I am up. Could you fix yourself some cereal while I jump into the shower? Sorry I overslept and now I don't have time to make you a hot breakfast.

"It's okay Momma. I can do it myself, Jamie yelled back.

After a few minutes, they said their goodbyes. Jamie was on the bus and Teresa was on her way to work. As she entered the door, Nate Bishop met her.

"Teresa, what are you doing here? Did you forget you are to be at Court today to see Judge Harris at 8AM?"

"Oh wow," flustered and embarrassed, Teresa said, "Yes, I forgot I think I can still be there by 8:15. I will be back as soon as it is over. Thanks Nate."

Nate Bishop had known Teresa for many years. She was his Head Seamstress and Administrative Assistant. She was very efficient, honest and dependable. Since her traumatic encounters of being kidnapped by her boyfriend, Ricky Clay, and falsely incarcerated for aiding and abetting in drug trafficking, she had not been the same. Often times she seemed to be daydreaming and distant. There were days she forgot deadlines, to send out memos, and her designs on the embroidered pillowcases lacked details, not to mention Nate had to prepare his own coffee most mornings. The mornings she forgot, Nate did not remind her. He was really worried about her. After all it had been six months now and she did not seem to be improving. He definitely did not want to terminate her and certainly hoped she would not resign, but he had to find a way to help her. Nate certainly understood the life altering ordeal. He tried not to remember his encounter with Ricky, and the attempt on his life, and how he barely escaped. Sometimes he would have nightmares of Ricky shooting him in the head, and just as Ricky was squeezing the trigger he would wake up, gasping for air. Sometimes he would urinate in the bed. Nate was extremely grateful that the

31

nightmares and bed wettings are not as frequent as they were six months ago. Lola, his wife, was very helpful and patient with him. They both understood and felt great compassion for Teresa. She had no one to help her get through the rough times at night when she is alone and vulnerable. At least they had each other.

"Perhaps an extended vacation or some professional help would motivate her to move on from her horrific nightmare," Lola suggested the night before.

"Yes, she seemed to be stuck. I will talk to her when she comes in tomorrow after court," he thought.

Nate was very grateful that Sal Tully had stepped in and worked extremely hard making things go smoothly for Paradise Pillows after Ricky was incarcerated. Sal was especially grateful that Nate had given him Ricky's position. He had to wear many different hats which often included parts of Teresa's job. Sal did not mind. He was exceptionally happy because he had a good job that was steady and dependable. He saved as much money as he could, because he and his wife, Carolyn, were finally expecting their first baby in a few months. He wanted to be the perfect father and husband.

****

Teresa arrived at the courthouse at 8:15AM. Just as she entered the court house, Esquire Troy Kennedy walked hurriedly over to her with obvious concern written on his face.

"Hello Teresa," extending his hand to shake hers.

"Hi Troy," as she shook his hand, trying hard to be polite.

"What's wrong?" she asked. "Am I in more trouble? Why are you here?"

Teresa had a tendency to ask many questions without waiting for an answer when she was annoyed.

"Whoa! Whoa! Whoa!" Troy said, smiling and giving Teresa the peace sign, suddenly remembering the open-handed knock-out slap she slammed Ricky Clay with in the courtroom.

"No Teresa, there is nothing wrong... you are not in any trouble... and I am here because I care. I just wanted to make sure everything is okay when you see Judge Harris. I thought you were to be here at 8:00AM to see him before court started."

Teresa tried to soften her expression because she realized she may need him after all. She *was* late and court had already started.

"Well, yes, I am sorry Troy; I am just upset that I am a little late. Now what should I do?"

"Well, let me see if I can get you in to see Judge Harris' clerk. She can do the papers to get your record expunged. Just wait here until I come back. Okay?"

"Do I really have a choice," Teresa said sarcastically.

Troy smiled and entered the "now in session" courtroom. In less than five minutes he was back holding the door for her to enter.

"Judge Harris wants to see you now."

Teresa hated to admit it, but she was really grateful that Troy was there. She did not know what was going to happen since she was late. She tried again to be gracious and thankful, but her body language was awkward and unappreciative as she strolled past Troy without saying thanks. Troy pretended not to notice her mean attitude and continued to smile as she pushed by him. Suddenly overwhelmed with fear, she realized she did not know what to do as she plunged into the courtroom. It appeared everyone's eyes were upon her. Troy stepped immediately in front directing the way, trying to shield her from their stares.

Judge Harris motioned them to approach the bench. Teresa stood once again, shaking and holding onto Troy's arm.

"Teresa Hayward, coming into my courtroom tardy says to me you don't respect me or my court and I don't tolerate that very well. But your attorney explained to the court that he detained you and he takes full responsibility for your tardiness. So, I will move on quickly to the issue at hand. Since you have not had any trouble with the law and you have been an upstanding citizen, your records will be expunged this day. Do you have any questions for me?"

"No, your honor and thank you. Thank you very much." she said trying to sound confident.

"All the best to you, young lady. If there is nothing else... glancing at Troy and pausing for a moment... Then you are dismissed. Have a nice day."

Troy gently touched Teresa's arm and led her out of the courtroom. Once outside, Troy said, "You don't have to thank me for anything. You don't have to explain why you would not return my calls, and you don't have to accept my invitation, but if I have been a friend to you then you can't say no this time. Would you please at least have a cup of coffee with me?"

Teresa was embarrassed and speechless. Why was she so rude to him? He has been nothing but nice since the first day she met him. He even lied for her to keep her from whatever Judge Harris did to those who came to his courtroom late.

"Okay, Well, I guess that is the least I can do. She said feeling a tinge of guilt. And yes, you do deserve a thank you. Thank you Troy and I appreciate everything you did."

Smiling, Troy suggested that they walk to the corner cafe a few blocks up the street. He touched her shoulder moving her to the inside of the walkway, as the perfect gentleman. They strolled along nonchalantly making casual conversation. As they entered the cafe, the smell of coffee, bacon and eggs reminded Teresa that she had not eaten breakfast because she had overslept. She was glad to take a seat and the waitress came right over with a fresh pot of coffee. They both settled in enjoying their cup of coffee. Troy was very engaging and caring. Teresa suddenly felt like a shy high school girl.

"Well Teresa, thank you for having a cup of coffee with me. Would you like to have a bite to eat as well?"

"If it is not too much trouble, yes I would like a bacon, egg and cheese on a hard roll. Troy laughed, "I like a lady who knows what she wants."

Teresa was a little perplexed at his statement.

"Well, he did ask what I wanted, so what was I supposed to say?" she thought.

Troy signaled the waitress and ordered two of the same. Teresa could hardly look up at him. Sensing her shyness,

Troy wanted her to relax. What can I talk about that will make her feel at ease....Jamie of course, he thought.

"So how is Jamie doing these days?"

"He is okay, just having a hard time trying to adjust to not having Ricky around. He is acting out in school and I really don't know quite what to do with him. I am thinking of taking a few days off from work when Spring break comes to get away for a while. Maybe that will help Jamie.

"It worked, she is ready to talk now," thought Troy.

"Where are you planning to go?" Troy asked sipping his coffee.

"I am not really sure yet. But I want to go someplace where I can relax and there's a lot of entertainment for Jamie," Teresa laughed, taking a bite of her sandwich.

"And you, Teresa? How are you adjusting?"

"I am fine," she lied. As a trained professional in his profession, Troy knew she was not being truthful.

"Please, Teresa, let me be your friend. I can help you. Don't push me away. I see you are hurting and Jamie has not healed because you have not healed. Would you mind if I come over sometime and take you and Jamie roller skating. I have been dying to see what I remember on the skates. I used to skate every weekend when I was a kid. It would be great. You can skate right?"

Teresa was stunned and speechless. She needed some time to process what he had just said. "Was he asking me out on a date?" Teresa never considered Troy, *her attorney*, being interested in her romantically. She certainly was not considering him. Aw shucks, he is at least ten or fifteen years older than me she thought. He is easy on the eyes though, very nicely dressed, smart, funny, very kind, and established but ....not Ricky Clay! Although I am not interested she reconsidered, but Jamie could definitely benefit from a positive male role model in his life.

"Yes, I haven't skated in a long time and Jamie has never gone skating before, but I am sure he would love to give it a try. He loves to fish.

"Okay, he's an outdoors kind of boy huh?"

"Yes, he and Ricky...stopping in the middle of her sentence, she looked away feeling very uncomfortable.

"Oh, that's okay. I know everything about his relationship with Ricky. Remember you told me. It is okay Teresa. I want you to feel free to talk about anything with me. I will never judge you. I just want to be here for you if you want to have a friend to talk to. I would love to be there for Jamie as well. It is not just a one-sided friendship. I could use a friend too - to share dinner or catch a movie or try my luck again at skating. Just a friend Teresa," he said smiling.

Teresa sat still again, unsure how to respond.

Troy added, "hey, don't look so serious. Yes, a vacation is definitely needed. You need to relax and have some fun. That's the best medicine for you now young lady," he teased.

She concurred.

"Yes, a nice get-away is just what the doctor ordered for me," smiling back at Troy. Teresa suddenly realized the time had once again escaped her and it was almost noon and Nate was probably wondering what had happened to her. She had to get back to work. She and Troy talked for nearly three hours and inwardly she really enjoyed talking to him. She had forgotten the trauma of her past for the moment.

"Troy, thank you again for breakfast and coffee, but I have to get back to work.

"Oh," Troy said, "one more thing, before I forget, I really wanted to talk to you about something that came to fruition after you met with Judge Harris six months ago. As your attorney, I need to advise you that you and Jamie have a bank account totaling about ten thousand dollars."

"What? What are you talking about?" She questioned, shaking her head in disbelief.

"Apparently, Ricky Clay had opened an account for Jamie in the amount of five thousand dollars and one for you also at Compton and Loan Bank over on East Main Street. If you want to take it out, all you have to do is go there and show your identification. As your attorney, I would advise you to take all the money out and put it in another account in your name only or in Jamie's name and make yourself his beneficiary. Right now, Ricky named his friends as beneficiaries if anything should happen to you or Jamie.

"What? Are you serious?" sighing deeply. Many thoughts began to run through her mind. Ricky was looking out for our future. He really does love us. Oh Ricky, I am so sorry I... Troy piped in interrupting her thoughts.

"Yes. It is true. The money is there at Compton and Loan.

She really wanted to be alone. She wanted to digest the news of Ricky loving her and Jamie so much that he opened an account for them. Oh how sweet of him, she marveled within herself.

Troy signaled the waitress who came over right away with the bill. Teresa seemed to be in deep thought.

"Okay young lady; let's get you back to work, interrupting her thoughts again.

They walked with purpose this time, getting back to their cars very quickly. Troy escorted Teresa to her car and thanked her again for having breakfast with him. "I will be in touch very soon. Spring break starts next week right?"

"Yes." she answered hurriedly getting into her car.

"Okay say hi to Jamie. I trust this time you will at least return my calls right?"

Teresa blushed and smiled. "Yes, I will" she said as she drove away.

CHAPTER 4

Michael cursed as he pulled over to the right side of the road just outside of Arkansas. He was angry at himself for not taking the time to get his truck serviced and now the engine light was on and the truck just stalled, making a ticking sound. Smoke seethed from under the hood.

"What now?" He thought.

Michael took a white handkerchief and tied it to the antenna to let other motorists know his truck was not working. It also was used as a sign to signal for help. Cars whizzed by at high rates of speed, causing the truck to rock. He thought it would be best to get back inside and stay put until a state trooper came.

Finally, an hour later, a state trooper came and radioed for a tow truck. Michael was very grateful when he arrived. It was hot, and with no air conditioning, it was extremely uncomfortable just sitting on the side of a major highway. The thermometer inside the truck rose quickly to 105 degrees, with the windows down.

State Trooper Auggie was very nice and offered Michael the comfort of his air conditioned cruiser while they waited for the tow truck. Michael gladly accepted. They talked about many things while they waited. Michael was most intrigued with Trooper Auggie's story of his relationship with Jesus. Trooper Auggie confessed he was a functional alcoholic and did not take care of his home or his wife. He was a trooper by day and a drunk by night. He had been a State Trooper for ten years before his wife left him. He came home from work one Friday evening and his house was completely empty, with the exception of his old army sleeping bag and a note saying, "I just can't take it anymore. I used to love you, but I don't know where the guy is that I once loved. Please don't bother looking for me until you find the man I fell in love with. Anna."

Michael thought of the scripture that he heard, *"If a man does not take care of his own, he is worse than an infidel."* Trooper Auggie had to be an infidel too, because he did not take care of his wife or his home. I gotta find out what that word really means.

Trooper Auggie admitted it was a blessing she left me, because I probably would have drank myself to death. But I know now, it had to be something big like my wife leaving me to get my attention. When she left, it was the turning point of my life. It had to be a part of God's plan to bring me to him. I cried out to God to deliver me and forgive me. The next Monday morning, I went to work and told my Captain I needed help and that I had a drinking problem and my wife had left me. I thought that was the best thing I could do, either get help or lose my wife

43

and my job. The Captain praised me for coming to him with such an admission. He quickly set up counseling through the department for employees who were struggling with certain challenges and gave me a leave of absence. I returned two years ago and I have been sober ever since. I know God heard me when I cried out to him. My Ol' drinking buddies would come around with their drinks. It was really hard at first, but I refused to drink with them and soon they stopped coming around because I always talked about Jesus to them.

"That's an amazing story," Michael said smiling. "Did your wife come back?"

"No, not yet, but we are seeing each other pretty regularly. I think she wants to make sure I am a changed man. She has been watching me very closely these last few months."

"I think she is waiting for you to ask her to renew your wedding vows again," Michael exclaimed.

"Oh, you mean like marry her again? Well, I have nothing to lose at this point," he thought.

"No doubt, that is what she is waiting for, Michael stated matter-of-factly.

"I never thought about that. You are probably right. I think I will even get her another ring and make it official again. He loved the idea and could not wait to see her the weekend. It was enough time to pick out a nice ring and even plan a weekend get-away with her, if she will go.

Trooper Auggie glanced in his rear view mirror. Well it has been nice speaking with you; I think I see the tow truck coming. It was the best forty-five minutes I spent on the highway in a while. Thanks for listening Michael; you must be my Angel that God sent to me to tell me how to get my wife back.

Michael laughed, yes; we were each other's Angel. You have helped me as well. By the way, do you know what the word "infidel" means?

"No, I can't say that I do Michael. Why do you ask?"

"Well a few days ago, I heard a preacher use the word and I did not know what it meant. I thought maybe you knew.

"No, but I will look it up when I get home. Thanks so much Michael for you have really been a blessing. By the way, have you ever asked Jesus to come into your heart?"

"Not really, but I do talk to Him sometimes."

"Let's make sure you are in the right place with Him. Just repeat this simple prayer with me and mean it with your whole heart and you will be saved. Okay?"

Michael was excited and a little confused, but was open to whatever Trooper Auggie recommended.

"Father God in Jesus' name, I believe that you died on the Cross for all of my sins and I now ask you to please forgive me of every sin known and unknown. I ask you to come into my heart and become Lord over my life. Teach me your ways and make me a vessel of honor for your glory in Jesus name, Amen."

Michael repeated every word. Now what, he thought. Trooper Auggie praised God and said, "Welcome to the family my brother. You are now born-again. Now you must get a Bible and read it and pray every day, find a good church and you will grow stronger and stronger in Jesus. Seek Him to know the plan He has for your life."

Michael felt excited and thankful that Trooper Auggie took time to tell him his story and lead him to Jesus. Now what does it mean to be saved he thought. They shook hands just as the tow truck pulled up behind his truck.

"Well," said Trooper Auggie, "I pray you can get the help you need with your truck. Take care of yourself and have a safe trip to New York. Here's my business card; if you are ever in this area again, give me a call."

"Sure thing," taking the card and here's mine also, Michael said, as he exited the police cruiser. Thanks so much and God's blessing with your wife this weekend. I may just give you a call when I get settled in New York. I want to know if your wife said "yes." They both laughed and shook hands again.

CHAPTER 5

It was around noon and Nate was leaving work to have lunch with his wife, Lola when he saw Teresa parking her car. He waited purposely for her to come into the office to speak with her, but before he could say anything, Teresa began to apologize.

"Nate, I am sorry for taking so long, I lost track of time and..."

"Oh, Teresa, it is okay, Nate said interrupting her. I just wanted to tell you that I am going to lunch with Lola. When I come back, I want us to talk about a nice vacation for you and Jamie. Spring break is coming up next week and it will be a perfect time to get away and have some fun. Think about it. We will talk when I come back."

Teresa hung her head in embarrassment.

"Thanks Nate. Yes sure, we can talk when you come back and say hello to Mrs. Bishop for me," avoiding direct eye contact.

Glad to be alone, Teresa quickly went to her workstation to reflect on everything. Ricky had opened a bank account for me and Jamie. I wonder if he mentioned it in any of the unopened letters I have been keeping in my safe. Is it really for me and Jamie? She thought of Troy and how kind he was, and how he wanted to be a part of Jamie's life, and, perhaps her life as well. She was so caught up in her thoughts she did not notice she had been in the same place thinking for over an hour. Nate had already returned from lunch. She was void of everything except the intimate, mindful moments of Ricky's, and Troy's kindness toward her until Nate called out to her.

"Teresa, Could you come in to see me?"

Embarrassed, she quickly responded. Yes, be right there, grabbing her note pad. Knocking lightly, she entered Nate's office. Nate waved her over to join him at the small conference table. Taking a seat, Teresa wondered what was next. He said he wanted to talk about a vacation for me. Is this going to be a permanent vacation? I know I have been a wreck these past six months and have not been my usual efficient self. *Oh, God, I can't lose my job. Please help me again.*

"Ah Teresa, I have been thinking. In a few days Jamie will be on spring break, so I am going to give you the rest of this week and spring break week off, with pay. I have two week's pay for you here in this envelope, just consider it a bonus. I really want you to get away and have some fun. Put everything behind you. I know this past six months have been really hard. I had a hard time getting back into the swing of things too. Ricky had a great effect on all of us. I truly understand, but it is all over now. You have to let it all go Teresa. I need you here and focused. You've been like family to me and Lola. We are here for you if there is anything we can do. She is always talking about how thankful she is for you bringing Ms. King to pray for me and how God used her to speak healing to my body. I too am forever grateful. That's why we are offering you and Jamie a cruise to Belize. It's a place where you can enjoy the sun and relax. Whatcha say Teresa?" pushing the envelope to her. "Just give Lola a call and give her the dates you want to travel. She will take care of everything."

"Nate, I don't know what to say. Thank you and I am sorry I have not been myself; but I can't take this, pushing the envelope back to him. I am certainly not deserving of your generosity and kindness."

"Now, I insist Teresa. Your leave starts now. Take this money and figure out where it is best for you and Jamie to go on vacation… and not another word young lady! Just be sure to tell your assistant, Leslie, what you want her to do in your absence, and be sure to tell her how you make my coffee," he chuckled. "I haven't been doing such a good job. It certainly does not taste like yours," laughing as he stood up and walked over to his desk.

Teresa blushed and stood as well. "You are a wonderful and kind man. I am very fortunate to work for you." Teresa gave him a hug and promised she would tell Leslie how to prepare his coffee. She decided to finish up a few things and sent out a memo advising every one of her extended vacation and the day of her return. As soon as all of her work was done, Teresa said farewell to Nate and headed home.

"What am I going to do the rest of the day. Today is Monday and spring break does not start until next Monday. Well, I can get caught up on some much needed cleaning, get rid of some of Jamie's clothes that he has outgrown, go to the Spa and get a body massage, pedicure and manicure; and just have a 'me' week."

Teresa had pretty much lost interest in all of those things she once did when she was seeing Ricky. She just did not seem to have a need to pamper herself; no one seemed to notice one way or the other, she thought.

"Well I will do some things this week for myself and try to figure out where Jamie and I can go. Belize sounds nice, but traveling out of the country alone with a nine year old does not sound like fun. I wonder if Momma King would like to go on vacation with us. I will ask her when I stop by later this evening to get Jamie," she said out loud. "Meanwhile, I will take a ride to Compton and Loan and check on the bank accounts that Ricky set up for me and Jamie."

Teresa arrived at the bank around two o'clock, and informed the teller she was there to close out the accounts. The teller asked her to please wait, she would be right back. She excused herself and came back with the Bank Manager, Mr. Wenzel.

"Teresa Hayward?" He inquired.

"Yes, I am Teresa Hayward."

"May I see your identification, please?" Teresa opened her purse and removed her Driver's License and handed it to him.

"Thank you Ms. Hayward. I am the Bank Manager, Mr. Wenzel, and I had the pleasure of setting up these accounts for Mr. Ricky Clay. He is such a nice man. I remember how much he loved you and your son—Jamie, right?"

"Yes," Teresa replied, not sure what she should say.

"How is he doing? I have not seen him in a while. Is he okay?"

"Yes, he is fine. I just need to close the accounts today," Teresa said. Mr. Wenzel nodded to the teller. I suggest we give you a Bank Check so you do not have to carry that amount of cash. Is that okay?"

"That will be just fine. Thank you Mr. Wenzel."

In a few minutes the teller came back with the Bank Checks. Teresa left Compton and Loan and quickly drove across town to her bank. She decided she would put all the money in

Jamie's name and make herself the beneficiary. Teresa sang along with the radio on the way to the bank. She was suddenly feeling great. After she made the deposit at the bank, Teresa went to Momma King's house to wait for Jamie.

CHAPTER 6

The tow truck driver explained that the nearest mechanic who could service his truck was about twenty miles out of the way.   Michael agreed, realizing he had no other choice, as he climbed into the truck.

"My name is Mike. Thanks for the tow."

"Jimmy Ray is my name. I am sorry but the only place around these parts that can work on your truck is about an hour away. The place does not look like much, and the owner is a little creepy, but he is an excellent mechanic."

They soon arrived at an old run down gas station five miles off the main highway, situated way back in the woods. It seemed to have more junk than gas. An old dog struggled to get up from his nap under the big shade tree. He wagged his tail and barked as if he was happy to see some new faces.

Looking around, Michael asked, "Are you sure there isn't another mechanic nearby?"

"No, said Jimmy Ray, "the next closest mechanic who can work on your Volvo truck is probably in Austin, Texas."

Michael frowned and accepted his dilemma. There is no one to blame but myself, he muttered under his breath.

Jimmy Ray called out, "Hey Charlie, I got you a customer and I am in a rush to get back. Where are you?"

Charlie yelled back, "be right there," but neither could tell where the yell came from as their eyes scanned the cluttered yard.

"Well I gotta run," said Jimmy Ray, "Charlie will take good care of you. He will be out in a minute. Take care and all the best to you.

Michael paid Jimmy Ray for his service as he unhooked his truck from the tow and left it in the "junk" yard. Michael realized he was far away from what seemed to be civilization and in the middle of nowhere. His only hope to get back to familiar territory was his truck or Jimmy Ray and now he was gone. Well, hopefully the mechanic can fix the problem and I will be on my way in a few minutes.

Charlie, the mechanic emerged from underneath the car that was sitting in plain sight, but yet unnoticed as Michael turned toward the noise he heard. Standing up wiping his greasy hands on a very filthy rag, he extended his hand to Michael smiling.

"Hey Charlie is the name boy, what can I do for you?"

Michael decided to ignore Charlie calling him a boy and took a few seconds to take it all in. Charlie had a huge wart that protruded on top of his nose, his face was dirty and greasy, his hair was bushy and uncombed and the color of a bright orange pumpkin. His mouth was stuffed with a big wad of chewing tobacco and just as Michael was about to shake his hand, he whipped his head in the direction of the dog and spat. The spit flew in the air about three feet landing in the dusty red clay, dirt rolling over and over. Michael hoped his face did not display the disgust he thought. Trying hard to smile, Michael managed to murmur, "Uh, I'm Mike and my truck needs servicing.

"That's a mighty fine machine you got there boy," Charlie said walking over to the truck and lifting up its hood.

"Uh Oh, did he just call me a boy again?" Michael thought to himself. I can see if I stay in this little country hick town there's gonna be a problem. I need to get outta here as soon as I can. I don't like the looks of this place and definitely don't like being called a boy.

"Thank you Charlie. It is a really good truck," trying to ignore his reference to him as a boy.

"What kind of business you do, boy?"

"Oh, I am sorry for not introducing myself properly. My name is Michael Hayden and most people call me Mike. I am just traveling through to New York. It's my company's truck I am using and I forgot to get it serviced before returning back to New York. Now, I am not sure what is wrong with it. I heard a ticking sound and then the engine died. I heard you are an excellent mechanic and the best in these parts. Why heck, I was even told you can fix and build anything when it comes to cars and you will be able to get me back on the road real quick."

Charlie knew he was a good mechanic, but he had not had a compliment in years. As a matter of fact, no one from out of town had been there in quite some time, only the locals came by for help.

"Really? Mike? You did say your name was Mike right? Now who told you that?" he asked, purposely calling him by his name.

"Yep, I just met a really nice state trooper named Auggie who said you were the best in the area and Jimmy Ray who brought me here said the same thing. He just left."

Charlie seemed really pleased, smiling showing his brown tobacco stained snaggleteeth. Only two teeth were visible, one on the top and one on the bottom.

"Oh my!" Michael thought. "He is just short of being completely repulsive. He has a face that only his mother could love."

People in the nearby town called him "Crazy Charlie" because of his appearance and his reclusive life style. He never married, nor did he have children. He was a loner indeed. He stayed to himself most of his life because he was always teased and made fun of because of his physical appearance. Even as an adult, the stares and whispering behind his back continued. He looked frazzled, creepy and disheveled. His escape from the stares and whispers was to isolate himself and work on cars. He was suddenly humbled by Michael's respect and mannerism.

"Ok, Charlie said, you can wait in the waiting room if you like, motioning him to the little small shack that Michael thought was the garage. I will check out whatever the problem is. Make yourself comfortable."

As he entered the shack, Michael thought, "Oh this is the real pits as he scowled looking at the dust and thin film of dirt that appeared to be on everything and in everyplace. In spite of all the dust, something was cooking and smelled really good. Michael quickly remembered he only picked at the breakfast Tavia had prepared for him earlier that morning. It was a strange and different scent; totally unfamiliar, but, yet it smelled delicious. An old table that held magazines was covered in dust in the center of the room. Several sheets hung across the room that seemed to separate that area from the waiting room. There was an old worn couch in front of the sheets. Across the room were two wrought iron chairs with a medium sized wrought iron table. An oversized, frayed black Bible that did not appear to be covered in dirt and dust laid in the middle. In the back of the room was an old potbelly stove with a cast iron pot that was slowly cooking something that was producing that scrumptious smell. In the corner of the little shack was a sleeping cot with matching covers that was neatly made. It was obvious that he lived there as well.

Disturbed by his present predicament, Michael reluctantly took a seat on the wrought iron chair. The only sensible thing to do was to pick up the only thing that was not full of dust...the Bible. Immediately upon opening it, his eyes glared on 2 Corinthians 6:15 with disbelief. It said: *"And what accord has Christ with Belial? Or what part has a believer with and infidel?"* Infidel...There is that word again, he thought. *"And what agreement has the temple of God with idols? For you are the temple of the living God. As God has said: I will dwell in them and walk among them. I will be their God, and they shall be my people. Therefore, Come out from among them and be separated, says the Lord. Do not touch what is unclean and I will receive you."* Michael dropped the Bible back on the table and jumped up from the chair dusting and wiping off his backside. This whole place is unclean, I gotta get outta here and separate myself. He quickly exited the little shack. Charlie was just heading toward the shack when Michael came bursting out, looking like he had just seen a ghost.

"Oh, Mike, Are you okay? Charlie asked.

"Uh yeah, I am okay, looking embarrassed. I just read something in your Bible and it kind of shook me up a bit. But I am okay."

"Yes, God's word will do that to you," he said unemotionally, making a mental note to ask him later what shook him. "But to get to the business we have here at hand concerning your truck; well, it is not good news," Charlie said. "The ticking sound you were hearing was the engine. There is no oil and the engine has sieged. You had to have been driving this machine for some time and did not check the oil. Now the engine is ruined and you are going to have to get another one.

Michael stood speechless shaking his head in total disbelief.

"Here's what I can do," Charlie informed. "I can rebuild this engine or I can order another one. If you want me to try to rebuild the engine it is going to take about four or five days provided I can get the parts I need. If I order the engine, it will take at least two weeks."

Michael's heart plummeted. He was flabbergasted and stuck. "This is a bad dream I am having, surely, I need to wake up now," he thought. "There are no hotels nearby, no one to call and even if he were able to reach someone, how would they be able to find him. Michael suddenly thought of Trooper Auggie's card he had in his pocket and quickly dismissed that thought because Trooper Auggie was going to spend the weekend winning his wife back. *God, why is this happening to me?" he questioned.*

CHAPTER 7

Momma King was surprised to see Teresa so early. "What's going on? How did everything go at court this morning? You did not go to work?" Momma King realized that she had asked several questions and she had not given her time to answer. "Oh, I am sorry honey, I was just overly concerned. Please, forgive me and allow me to give you an opportunity to answer me, pausing to laugh at her anxiousness.

Teresa chimed right in nonstop. "Momma King, you would not believe what happened today. I forgot I was supposed to go to court because I overslept, and out of habit I went straight to work. Nate reminded me when I got to work of my court date and I left immediately but arrived to court late. Troy Kennedy was there and got me in to see the Judge. My records were expunged. I ended up having breakfast with Troy who told me that Ricky had put ten thousand dollars away in a bank account for me and Jamie!!

"What? Wait a minute! Slow down child; let me take this all in. Come and have a cup of tea with me and tell me everything. Jamie will not be here for at least another hour. So, you had breakfast with Troy? Wow, that is really nice. He is such a nice man and he is single too." Teresa shrieked and waved Momma king off.

"No, no, no" Teresa said. "I am not interested. He really is nice and kind, but I am not interested. He is at least 10 or 15 years my senior, like a father image, but I did tell him he could come by sometime and take me and Jamie skating.

"Really," Momma King said, with great excitement in her voice. Oh, girl, don't count him out because he is a few years older. That means he is more mature and knows what he wants in life. He is looking for a cute little thing like you to hang on his arm and that is okay. He is a well-established attorney, he is born-again and he certainly is easy on the eyes... before you rule him out. Pray. Sometimes God will send us what we really need and because it is not wrapped in blue like we expect, we totally disregard the package. So tell me. Ricky Clay really left you and Jamie ten thousand dollars?"

"Yes, Momma King. Troy told me the money was there. It was discovered when they investigated Ricky's finances. Troy suggested I close the account because some of Ricky's friends were listed as beneficiaries. I went to Compton and Trust this afternoon and closed out the account and put it all in Jamie's name at my bank for his education."

"Praise God, Teresa, the Bible says, the wealth of the wicked is stored up for the righteous!" Momma King added smiling.

"Momma King, Ricky is not wicked. He really is not a wicked man." Teresa said protectively.

Surprised by Teresa's defensive tone, Momma King did not respond. Momma King knew she was still struggling with Ricky being incarcerated and absent from her life.

Quickly changing the subject, Teresa said, "Oh Momma King, Nate gave me the rest of the week off and all of spring break. "In fact," she said, reaching for her purse pulling out the envelope Nate gave her, "Nate and Mrs. Bishop gave me this money to take me and Jamie on a nice vacation. I was thinking Momma King, when was the last time you went on a vacation? Would you like to go on vacation with us?"

"Well, that sounds marvelous my child. I would love to but I can't go during the spring break because I have to teach a class on the gifts of the Holy Spirit. I was hoping you and Jamie would be able to come to the church for the class. It is going to be every night for nine nights starting next week."

"Why nine nights?" Teresa asked.

"One night for each of the gifts, there are nine gifts of the Holy Spirit.

"Really!" Teresa said. "I would love to go to learn about that."

Okay, this is what we can do. I will keep all of my notes and we can have a little Bible study right here when you guys come back. How does that sound?"

"Yes, Momma King, that sounds great. I really have to get my life back on point. Nate hinted today that I was not the same and insisted I take some time off to get myself together. Maybe Bible study is the answer.'

"Praise God," Momma King thought to herself, "perhaps now she can get her healing. It was the first time Teresa even acknowledged that her life was in disarray."

"Have you decided where you are going on vacation?" Momma King asked.

"No, not yet. I will give it some thought tonight and try to figure out something. The Bishops wants to send me to Belize with all expenses paid. I don't want to go out of the country, so I need to find someplace not too far from here. Any suggestions?" she implored.

"Actually, no, but I can give it some thought," she said. "That was so nice of Mr. and Mrs. Bishop. They really love you Teresa. Oh dear," she said, glancing at the clock on the wall, "the time slipped by fast, it's about time for Jamie to get off the bus."

"Oh, I will go meet him," Teresa said. "He will be surprised to see me."

Arriving at the bus stop a few minutes later was just as Teresa predicted. Jamie was surprised.

"Ma! What are you doing here and where's Momma King?' He questioned as he jumped off the last of the bus steps to give her a hug.

Teresa was concerned when she saw him with dried tears that stained his face and a tiny amount of dried blood in his left nostril. "Jamie, what happened? Were you fighting again?" She asked looking him square in his little chubby face.

"Yes Mama, Tyler missed the ball in gym today and we lost the game. I was so mad at him I pushed him down. He scraped his knee and got up and hit me in the nose. Ricky told me to never back down from a fight, even if I start it. I should finish it."

"What? No, Jamie, that is not the right thing to do. Come on let's talk about it with Momma King. You can't continue to fight with other kids because they don't do what you want them to do. That is being a bully. I am off the rest of the week and I am going to your school tomorrow. You are going to apologize to Tyler. Jamie Hayward you are getting way out of control, and I am not happy with you fighting and being a bully!" She thought, "What has happened to my sweet little

Jamie? Where is he? It seems like hostility has taken him over since Ricky left. I must get him in to see a professional if this vacation does not help. I am sure there will be another message on the answering machine from your teacher about your behavior, and I will have to go to your school again," she scolded as she entered Momma Kings' house.

"Look at the big heavy weight fighter we have here Momma King," pointing at Jamie's face. "What are we going to do with him?" Teresa said, with contempt.

"Fighting again Jamie?" Momma King asked stretching her arms out to him for a hug.

"Yes ma'am, Tyler made us lose the game today. I don't like to lose," he cried.

"Come on let's get cleaned up," motioning him to the bathroom.

After washing Jamie's face, Momma King said, "Come on. Let's have some snacks and talk a bit."

Jamie climbed onto the kitchen chair, waiting for his milk and cookies.

"Jamie, you know your mother and I love you very much. And you know Jesus loves you too, right?" said Momma King.

"Yes ma'am," his eyes grew wide with excitement. He loved talking with Momma King about Jesus and Bible stories. Teresa saw the enthusiasm on Jamie's face and decided she wanted to hear as well and took a seat on the opposite side of the table.

"When Jesus came on the earth as a young boy, there were a lot of people that tried to bully Him because he did not do everything they wanted Him to do. Jesus could have beaten them all up, but He was a true gentleman. He did not want to fight them because He wanted to please his father and make his father proud. Just like your momma and I want you to make us proud by not fighting and being a bully," Momma King said gently.

"But I don't have a father, he whined. Ricky was like my father and he is gone now and I don't have a father like all of my friends." Teresa's heart sank as she witnessed Jamie's pain.

"Oh yes, you do sweetie. You have a father and a big brother." Jamie frowned, clearly lacking understanding. "God is your father and Jesus is your big brother. You can't see them like you can see me and your momma, but you can feel them. Remember when I anointed you with oil and prayed for you and you began to feel warm and tingly inside?" Jamie nodded his head excitedly as he reminisced.

"Well that is Father God letting you know He is with you. Sometimes you can feel him and sometimes you may not feel Him, but you must know that He is always with you and He loves you and He loves Tyler too. Father God and your big brother Jesus are not proud when you fight Tyler because he did not do what you wanted him to do."

"I am sorry Momma King and Mama," whined Jamie. "I guess I need to tell Tyler I am sorry too, right?"

"Yes of course, but there is someone else you need to say you are sorry to. Do you know who that is?" Momma King asked.

"No Ma'am." Jamie answered.

"Father God and your big brother Jesus!" Momma King exclaimed.

"But they already know because they are always with me right?" Jamie said, not completely understanding.

"Well yes, but wouldn't you feel left out if I only talked to your mother and completely ignored you?" she answered.

Jamie smiled shyly and said, "Sorry God, sorry Jesus. I want to make you both proud of me, just like Ricky. He was proud of me too, but I must have done something that made him not proud of me because he left me and Mama." He began to cry.

"Now, now, Jamie, don't cry, let's pray," as she took their hands and sat at the head of the table. *"Dear Father God, In Jesus' name, I know you see the pain and hurt in little Jamie's heart. He feels rejected and abandoned. He is acting out his hurt in school by fighting and bullying his classmates. Lord he is too young to understand some things that are happening in his life right now, but I know you know how to turn this situation around. Give us back the Jamie that loves everyone. The Jamie that is kind-hearted and gentle. So, God, by the power and the authority you have given me by the blood of Jesus and the power of the Holy Spirit, I break every unhealthy and ungodly soul tie that has formed in Jamie's life through the spirit of manipulation and deception. I break the power of rejection and low self-esteem and anger that was formed from this unhealthy soul tie. I decree and declare total freedom from the damage of this unhealthy impartation and I speak deliverance, healing and total restoration over his life NOW in Jesus' name. Amen."*

Teresa sat with tears flowing down her face as well. Momma King discerned that she too was struggling with the same issues as Jamie. Momma King moved quickly to the china cabinet and took out her scented frankincense holy oil and anointed both of their heads as she prayed in tongues over them. Tears streamed down both of their faces as they surrendered to the power of God.

CHAPTER 8

Charlie was born-again but did not go to church because he did not want to be around a lot of people. He always felt they were laughing at him. Pastor Jo understood and often stopped by after church in the evenings and had Bible study and prayer with him. Charlie felt Pastor Jo was the only one who was sincere and actually practiced what he taught from the Bible. Charlie deemed him to be a real friend. Remembering what Pastor Jo shared with him, he was moved with compassion for Michael as much as he could be. Not interacting with people on a regular basis caused Charlie to be a little rough around the edges.

"Now listen here Mike, you will be here for a while and the way we live around here is nothing like the city life of a city boy. Come on in," waving Mike to follow him back into the house. "There is nothing more I can do on the truck. I should have several parts coming in tomorrow and I will be able to work on it some more, but in the meantime, get used to your new home for a few days. Now, it is not as fancy as you are accustomed to, but if you don't like being in here you can sleep in your truck." Charlie remembered Mike running out of his house as if he saw a ghost. Well whatever Mike saw or was thinking, I am not going to ask him and I am gonna try my best to be nice to him, Charlie thought. Pastor Jo's message was still strong in his mind from their last Bible study. Mike stood awkwardly by the door, contemplating if the truck was the better of his options.

"Sit anyplace you like, I am going to finish cooking dinner." Charlie walked over to the sink and poured a heavy powder on his hands which lathered up rather nicely. He washed and rinsed. He repeated the same process two times with little improvement to the naked eye. His hands still looked dirty as Michael tried to take it all in.

Michael moved back over to the wrought iron chair and table that held the Bible and brushed lightly at the dust and took a seat.

"Welcome to my humble abode. It is a little dusty and cluttered and I am not the best housekeeper," Charlie said, chuckling, "but it is mine and it's paid for."

Michael was speechless. He strained to smile. He did not know what to do or say. Michael looked away and down at the Bible that still laid open on the table.

"Oh come on Mike, cat got your tongue? You are going to be stuck here for a few days. Let's make the best of it okay?" Michael barely nodded. "Come on in here and wash your hands for dinner. I cooked enough for two days, so I have plenty. You must be plenty hungry by now."

"Yes," said Michael as he walked over to the deep sink. "I am pretty hungry. It smells really good and I appreciate your hospitality," he finally uttered. Michael could not help but be curious as to what was that unfamiliar but pleasant odor that filled the little shack. In a few minutes, they had removed the dusty magazines and Bible from the wrought iron table. Charlie took one plate that was made of silver tin that had many dings on it for himself. He proudly set an old blue plate with faded flowers etched in it before Michael, each plate consisting of a piece of dark meat, a green leafy vegetable and a long unpeeled baked sweet potato. Michael recognized the potatoes, but the rest he did not have a clue as to what it was, but it did smell delicious. Michael realized he had no other choice but to try to look past the untidy shack and the countenance of his new companion. On the other hand, Charlie was euphoric to share his dinner with Michael. "Let us pray now," he said, bowing his head. *"O Father of the Heavens and the Earth, You are always faithful to provide for me and I thank you O Father of the Heavens and the Earth for giving me a house guest, because it gets lonely out here sometimes. I know you always have a plan and a purpose for everything you do, including Mike's truck breaking down and allowing our paths to cross. I thank you for that. Thank you for allowing me to catch this muskrat yesterday and it is now for our dinner tonight. Thank you for the swamp cabbage and the sweet taters. Now let us enjoy the food you gave us and please stay and eat with us too that we will have great fellowship. In your name…Jesus the Christ. Amen."*

Michael suddenly wasn't hungry anymore and actually felt ill and nauseous. Muskrat and swamp cabbage? *"Oh, God please help me. What could possibly be your plan to have me here with this crazy looking lunatic? This awful forsaken place and no place to escape and now my dinner is Muskrat and swamp cabbage? Oh God in heaven, please wake me up now, I know this is a bad dream,"* he concluded, as he prayed silently within himself.

Charlie smiled as he tore off a piece of the meat and sopped it in the juice with his fingers. "Come on boy, let's eat as he filled his mouth. Cat really does have your tongue huh?"

Michael sat dumbfounded. He did not want to be disrespectful or ungrateful, so he lowered his eyes and focused on the sweet potato. The meat appeared to be very tender and it smelled delicious, but it was hard for Michael to get past what Charlie said it was. And his one tooth on the top and one on the bottom, the carrot top colored hair and the large wart on his nose made it almost impossible to even eat looking at him. Michael decided to focus on what looked familiar to him, the potato but that was difficult as well as he tried to peel the hot potato with his bare hands, dropping it back on the plate.

"Oh, excuse my manners," Charlie said, realizing he had not given Michael any eating utensils. The truth of the matter was he ate with his fingers most of the time and he only had two metal spoons, one had a broken handle, a butter knife and a butcher's knife, which he used to cut and skin his meat and a large wooden spoon and fork he used to stir his stews. Charlie smiled as he gave Michael the metal spoon and the old discolored butter knife.

"Here now that should help" he said as Michael reluctantly accepted.

Charlie watched Michael very closely and sensed his discomfort. Trying to make light of it, Charlie said, "So you believe in God, boy?"

"Yes, I believe in God," Michael said gazing intently and feeling frustrated at his situation and now being disrespected.

"I am deeply humbled by you sharing and helping me, but I thought I told you my name is Michael and most people call me Mike. Not boy!!

"Oh yes, of course, I am sorry if I offended you," Charlie said remembering the message his pastor shared with him earlier in the week. "I believe God used my pastor to prepare me for your visit," stuffing his mouth with more food.

"Really, how so?" inquired Michael taking a big bite of his sweet potato.

"Well last week, Pastor Jo came here to have Bible Study with me. I don't like to go into town to church because some people sneer and make comments that are not very nice to me. Pastor Jo cared enough about me to come here and teach me the Bible. He is a real man of God. The things he taught me last week helped me to understand that God loves everybody. I just realized I did to you what others have done to me and I am ashamed. Please forgive me. I have disrespected you by calling you a "boy" because I was taught that "coloured" men should always be referred to as a "boy" because they are inferior and can never be equal to the white man. When I saw you here standing in my yard with that fancy truck, it just took me back to the way I was raised, that you should not have that much success. I should have never judged you by your outward appearance or the color of your skin."

Michael was humbled by his lucidity. "Really! You were actually taught this?"

"Yep, but I know now that according to God's Word it is wrong, and I guess my parents taught me that because their parents taught them the same as well. Pastor Jo said once you know the truth the truth will make you free. Since he has been coming to share the Bible with me I have been set free from a lot of things, but I sometimes still mess up and don't do the right

76

thing, he said feeling convicted for calling him a boy. Pastor Jo taught me what is written in James the 2nd chapter. It talks about being prejudice and having a haughty personality. See right here, as he picked up the Bible and turned to the book of James and began to read to Michael. Michael again was amazed at how well Charlie could read.

He read: *"My friends, as believers in our Lord Jesus Christ, the Lord of Glory, you must never treat people in different ways according to their outward appearance. Suppose a rich man wearing a gold ring and fine clothes comes to your meeting, and a poor man in ragged clothes also comes. If you show more respect to the well-dressed man and say to him... have this best seat here, but say to the poor man, ...stand over there, or sit here on the floor by my feet...then you are guilty of creating distinctions among yourselves and of making judgment based on evil motives. Listen, my dear friends! God chose the poor people of this world to be rich in faith and to possess the kingdom which he promised to those who love him. But you dishonor the poor! Who are the ones who oppress you and drag you before the judges? The Rich! They are the ones who speak evil of that good name which has been given to you. You will be doing the right thing if you obey the law of the Kingdom, which is found in the scripture, "Love your neighbor as you love yourself." But if you treat people according to their outward appearance, you are guilty of sin, and the law condemns you as a lawbreaker."* It is also written somewhere, I forgot where it is that says, *"we look on the outward appearances of man, but God looks on the heart."*

"Wow," Michael said, "I am impressed. How long have you been studying with your pastor?"

"It has been a little over nine months now. I read, study and pray every night after I finish dinner and every morning before I start my day working on cars. I used to feel lonely out here, but now I always feel God is right here with me, but it is still nice to have a person in the flesh to talk to every now and then. It feels good to know that He promised to never leave me nor forsake me. But, in spite of my closeness with God, I am still struggling with some things. The way to conquer the flesh is by not letting it do what it wants to do, but discipline it and *DO* according to what the word of God tells us to do. That is the hardest part. The flesh always wants to do opposite of what God wants us to do. When I saw you standing in my yard with your fancy truck and dressed nicely, I felt you did not deserve to have that amount of success because of your race. My carnal and fleshly nature rose up and immediately wanted to disrespect you by calling you boy. Then I kept hearing Pastor Jo in my head.

"Pastor Jo told me something that I will never forget. It gave me an insight I never knew before, but I still struggle to apply it sometimes." He said, 'Genesis chapter 1:26 and 27, explains that we are created in God's image. God's image includes every human race; Caucasian, African, Asian, Indian, Arab, Jew, Mexican, Chinese, etc. We see them as different races, but the reality is that they are really *different ethnicities* of the human race. If God's love is unbiased, then we the human race that is created in His image must be the same. We must love each other regardless of race, creed, color, or national origin. If we treat a person with insolence, we are mistreating a person created in God's image and are hurting somebody that God loves. Wow, what a revelation that was for me," he said, choking back his tears.

"I am guilty too Michael said bashfully. When I saw you I looked at your outward appearance and judged you as well because of where you live. The way you look is different from what I am accustomed to, but that is no reason for me to think more highly of myself. Even with this food, I never had muskrat or swamp cabbage before, but when you are hungry everything is good. I remember my grandmother's favorite saying was "hard times will make a monkey eat red peppers and love it."

Charlie threw his head back, roaring in laughter as if that was the funniest thing he had ever heard.

"I must admit, I don't think I would have ever tried it, but I was really hungry and the smell was mouth-watering. It tasted even better. Thank you, Charlie."

Charlie continued to laugh revealing his two hideous teeth. "Michael, it's no problem, I am happy to share what God has given me."

This was the first of six nights they would spend together. They shared their hearts and prayed together. Michael ate food he never thought would ever be a part of his diet and had to admit Charlie was a pretty good cook. Foods like Bullfrogs, opossums, snapping turtles, fried Hoe Cakes, Cracklings Cornbread, boiled peanuts and black strapped molasses. Michael was introduced to Jesus in a more intimate way. He learned more of Jesus' character and what he did on Calvary's cross. He understood the purpose of the Cross and why Jesus died. It was no longer a hearsay experience. This was a real personal experience that was as real as his predicament. "Was this part of God's plan?" he wondered.

It was close to nine o'clock when Charlie got up to tidy the table and clean the dishes. Michael offered to help, but Charlie insisted, no way. They continued to talk about God and how much He loved everyone in the whole wide world. But yet, some will never know. Michael was suddenly overwhelmed with how unworthy and undeserving he was and yet God still loved him. He began to feel the presence of God and began to weep and repent. Charlie joined in and turned on his record player and played praise and worship music. It was pretty obvious that Charlie listened to those songs on a regular basis.

He sang every song and his voice wasn't too bad either. He could at least hold a note and stay in tune. He is truly full of surprises, Michael thought. What a blessing to be here with him. This whole day has been amazing. I am convinced now that God did allow all of this to happen and he does have a plan for my life. He learned a lot from Charlie during the six days he stayed. They danced, praised and worshipped God.

It was nearly midnight when Charlie went to his nicely made bed and pulled out a drawer from underneath his bed. There was extra blankets and linen that was packed neatly in the drawer. Charlie took out a pillow and three matching pieces of bedding, a blanket and sheet and a pillow case, placing them on the old couch across the room. "Well, you can sleep here if you want to, or you take your blanket and pillow to sleep in your truck. I know it is not the best but you are welcome," said Charlie.

"Ah my friend, we just learned that we are no better than the other, right? So if it is good enough for you and Jesus then it is surely good enough for me because Jesus definitely lives here," Michael said smiling, "and thanks for your warm hospitality."

Over the course of the next six days, Michael and Charlie connected like no other. They stayed up each night to almost midnight with Charlie teaching Michael scriptures and parables in the Bible. It was an amazing six days and Michael was like a sponge. He soaked up everything, and of course he learned that an infidel was an unbeliever and to not believe in God is eternal damnation. Michael felt relieved to know that he is a believer now, before he never gave it much thought. This experience was truly enlightening and Michael felt great joy and an inner peace he never knew. He assisted Charlie as much as possible. He occasionally pumped gas for the once in a while customer and assisted Charlie as he worked on his truck, by handing him different tools as needed. They continued to talk about God and His amazing grace, and love at every opportunity.

CHAPTER 9

Teresa rushed into her apartment as the phone was ringing. "Hello? Hello? Oh, well, whoever it is they can call back if they really want to reach me. Looking at the flashing light, Teresa yelled at Jamie, I have a message on the voice mail and I bet it is your school calling me. Jamie came closer looking angry as he eyed the flashing light.

"Mama I told you at Momma King's house I am sorry, now what else do you want me to do?" Jamie snapped.

"Oh, you talking back to me now and being disrespectful?

"No M'am, but I already…

"Go to your room Jamie and stay there until I decide what to do with you." Jamie stomped off sucking his teeth.

Frustrated and annoyed, Teresa pushed the button to hear the recording. There were two messages. Yep, just as she suspected, Mr. Dillon, the school principal had called asking her to come in because there was a situation that transpired today involving Jamie, and they would like to discuss it with her. He asked if at all possible, could she please accompany Jamie to school tomorrow morning.

Well, that will not be a problem now since Nate has given me the rest of the week off and another week off to take a vacation someplace, she thought to herself.

The next voice was very familiar "Teresa, it is Troy Kennedy and I just wanted to say thank you for having breakfast with me today. I really enjoyed your company. You said you were thinking of going on a vacation someplace with Jamie and I have a wonderful suggestion for you. I will call you back a little later. Okay, bye."

"Yeah, Yeah, Yeah, call me later," she said mockingly. "I got a more serious issue to deal with right now."

Teresa went into her bedroom and decided to pray for herself and Jamie. Momma King was always praying for me and Jamie, perhaps it is time for me to grow up in Jesus. I have to seek God for myself. Teresa sat down on the ottoman at the foot of her bed. *"Okay, God, first of all I want to say thank you. Thank you for coming into my life and being a good and close friend. As my Savior and close friend, I need your help. I don't know what to do. My son is hurting badly because I exposed him to a toxic relationship that has gone ghastly wrong. How can I help him? Please give me wisdom and guide me by your Holy Spirit as to what to do to heal myself and Jamie. I am hurting too. I have a hard time concentrating and I am still in love with Ricky and I feel I am living a life that is full of lies and deceit. I pretend to be okay around people that I love, but I know they see me still trying to find my way back from this life changing experience with Ricky. God, as you already know, I have all those letters in the safe from Ricky that I have not read because I am afraid to face the truth. Please help me. I really need you to intervene in my life. I need you Jesus. Please advise me. Thank you so much Jesus. Amen.*

Teresa sat still for a few minutes and remembered she had sent Jamie to his room. She decided she would go to his room to talk to him. As she approached Jamie's room, she heard Jamie crying and calling out to Ricky, she entered and sat on Jamie's bed and pulled him into her arms.

"Oh, Jamie, don't cry, it is going to be alright. I know you miss Ricky and I do too, but I want to tell you that I know how you feel. A long time ago when I was a little girl about your age, my mommy, your grandma Lena, left me. She promised she was going to come back in six months but she never did. I was hurt and angry with her for a long time. Then, when I had you, your father whom I loved very much left me too. I was devastated and lonely until I met Ricky. He helped me to grow up and let go of my past pain and fears. Even though Ricky is no longer here, I feel a lot stronger because of the good and happy times we had together. So, I want you to remember the good times you had with him just in case he never comes back. Remember how much he loved you and the fun you had with him fishing and doing 'guy stuff' Okay?"

"Yes m'am" he said, sitting up and wiping his eyes. Now, if I, myself, could believe what I just told Jamie she thought, I could be healed and whole too.

"You are growing into a really fine young man and it is very important for you to do well in school like you did before. Ricky would want that." Teresa wondered if she had handled this situation correctly. The fact that she finally confronted some of her past hurts and talked about it was therapy for her too.

"C'mon Jamie, let's get cleaned up and get ready for dinner. I love you so much and everything is going to be alright. I think we both need a break. We are going to take a little vacation next week."

"Really Mom, where are we going? Huh? Huh?"

"I am not sure yet. Let's talk about it later this evening. I have to get some food on the table and check your homework. C'mon Jamie, you can help me make the salad."

"Okay, said Jamie, trying hard to smile to soothe his momma.

CHAPTER 10

Momma King had just settled down for the night, just pinned up her hair, put on her night gown and her favorite cold cream on her face when she realized she was out of her favorite tea. With everything that was going on with Jamie fighting in school, it had completely slipped her mind. "Oh well, I have to have my tea!" she declared. Now frustrated that she would have to get dressed and cleaned up again just to go out. She would never leave her home in hair rollers or with anything out of place. It wasn't vanity; it was just the way she was. She would always say, "I would rather take the few extra minutes to make a nice appearance than to go out and be embarrassed. Your first impression is the lasting impression. You can never do it over again, so do the best you can the first time." She lived by that motto.

It was about 5:30PM when Momma King arrived at the All In All Supermarket. She quickly parked her car and got a shopping cart and decided she would pick up a few more things in addition to the tea. "Okay, I will go over to the produce area and get a few bananas, grapes, ginger and fresh pineapple; Then I will get the Black English Tea that I love so much and get back home," speaking out loud to herself. I will have a nice hot cup of tea while reading my Bible tonight, she thought. Just as she turned the aisle and picked up the box of tea, someone behind her said, "Well, Hello there, Ms. Joni King!"

Momma King turned around suddenly, half recognizing the voice, and stared into a face that was vaguely familiar. He quickly extended his hand. Momma King was confused. "Who is this man that knows her complete name? He does look somewhat familiar but how does he know me?" She cautiously extended her hand. He graciously took her hand and with a half bow, kissed the back of her hand and flashed a full smile that showed well-cared-for teeth that seemed to light up his face. The creases around his eyes seemed to disappear as well. Flattered but frightened, Ms. King snatched her hand away with a look of great disapproval.

"I am sorry, but do I know you?" she confessed.

"I am so sorry, but I always remembered you and prayed for the day that I would meet you again, outside of my courtroom. And today is the day God so graciously answered my prayers and allowed our paths to cross. I am Les Harris. If my memory serves me correctly, you came to my court room with a young lady named Teresa Hayward about 6 months ago.

"Oh my, well of course, you are Judge Harris. Yes, of course I remember. I also remember one of your courtroom officers' threatened to put me out if I did not take my seat after

Teresa hit Ricky Clay in the head. The both of them enjoyed a good hearty laugh.

"Yes, I will never admit this to anyone else but you... he deserved every bit of that, he whispered lowly. They both laughed again.

"That was a day I never will forget. It was the day I first saw you in my court room. Do you believe in fate Ms. King?"

"Yes, I do" she replied.

"Well, I do too, especially when I first saw you. I knew something happened in me and I asked one of the courtroom officers to get your name. I prayed every night for the past 6 months that I would get the opportunity to meet you again. I am overwhelmed with gladness that God has allowed this to happen. I just left from work and stopped by to get some Butter Pecan ice cream, which I just seemed to have a taste for and lo and behold, here you are!"

Momma King was almost speechless, but could not give up the opportunity to share how she also came to the market, which was not the usual for her either at this hour.

They laughed and talked well over thirty minutes as if they had known each other for years. The conversation was light yet interesting and fun. Momma King had not enjoyed a man's company since her beloved Harold died in the tragic car accident eight years ago. She and Judge Harris quickly checked out of the supermarket. He insisted that he pay for the things she had to purchase as well. Momma King was determined to pay for her things until Judge Harris told her she could repay him by making him a nice home cooked meal, which she could not say no to. After that was settled they continued their conversation as they walked to her car.

"Oh my, it's almost 7PM! Momma King exclaimed. I must get back home. It is true I suppose, time flies when you are having fun," she said, smiling as he opened her car door.

Yes, Joni, this is just the beginning of some good wholesome fun. I am elated to have met you again and this time, let's exchange numbers so you can let me know when I can come over for dinner, he said as he winked his eye at her.

Oh, okay as she reached in her glove compartment and took out a pad and scribbled her name and number. Momma King smiled as she glanced in the mirror. She thanked God inwardly for taking the extra minutes with her appearance before leaving her home. Judge Harris quickly scribbled his home number on the back of his business card. "I am looking forward to hearing from you real soon he said handing her his card. Momma King replied, "no, no, no… you must call me…and then we can set up a time.

"Okay, I will be calling you later this evening.   "Is that okay?"

"Yes, that will be fine, Momma King said.

"Thank you and get home safe," as he closed her car door.

"Yes, thank you and you as well," she said smiling, feeling like a young high school girl.

CHAPTER 11

Teresa cleaned up the remains of dinner and had just accepted Jamie's challenge to a game of Checkers when the phone rang.

"Hello" she said.

"Hello, Teresa. It's Troy Kennedy. Did I catch you at a bad time?

"Well, I was just getting ready to play a game of Checkers with Jamie," she replied.

"Okay, I will only be a minute. I just wanted to say thanks again for meeting with me today and I have a suggestion for you. You said you wanted to get away for a nice vacation with Jamie, so I would love to invite you and Jamie as my guests to our Harlem's Country Club for Attorneys' (HCCA) and families. It has everything! It is like your own paradise island with tons of things to do for entertainment. Is it okay if I stop by your place tomorrow to bring you brochures and literature on what it has to offer? I think you will be pleasantly surprised."

"Mom, Come on. I set up the board already. Which color do you want? Red or black?" Jamie yelled across the room.

Excuse me Troy, Could you hold on a minute?" Teresa implored, as she covered the mouth piece of the phone to speak to Jamie.

"Jamie, I will be with you in a minute. Please go and brush your teeth and get ready for bed and I will be ready for you when you are finished. And I want the red checkers." Jamie sucked his teeth and shuffled off to the bathroom.

"Yes, Troy, thank you for calling back and yes, that would be fine. I will be home most of the day.

Okay great, I will stop by around 6PM if that is okay and I will bring dinner. How about Chinese Food, or Pizza or better yet, how about dinner out? You, me and Jamie?"

No, I like the first suggestion best. I am not picky, so surprise us with whatever you have a taste for. Troy smiled, pleased at her answer. "I do like a lady who knows what she wants. I will see you at 6PM," he said teasingly.

Teresa could not believe she accepted his invitation so easily. She thought... "Well it was nice having him around when I was in trouble, it was nice having breakfast with him this morning and it was nice when he rescued me from Judge Harris' punishment for being late... whatever that was, and it was nice... Oh stop it!" She scolded herself. Let's just see what he has to offer, trying to convince herself that it was a good idea.

CHAPTER 12

In spite of all the mishaps of Nate Bishop's business, Paradise Pillows continued to thrive and flourish. Ricky Clay worked hard establishing Nate's business, even though he had his own agenda so he could smuggle drugs and establish the illegal business which sent him to prison. It was not all bad, considering Nate's business had never been more productive. Nate realized he had to promote Teresa's assistant, Leslie Stamford, to assist him in Teresa's absence. He decided to send her to New Jersey to meet one of Paradise Pillow's long-time buyer, Dennis Hayes. Usually Teresa would take the trip to New Jersey. She would make the sale and return the same day, because she wanted to get back home to Jamie and Ricky. Nate would always insist that she take advantage of the opportunity and stay a couple of nights, but she never did. Unlike Teresa, Leslie was thrilled to take the trip and the opportunity to enjoy the luxury of a five star hotel for two nights. It was a blessing for her.

It was around noon when Leslie arrived and checked into the Edison Hotel. The one hour drive was just long enough for her to drool for the Jacuzzi, Sauna and other amenities the hotel offered before meeting Dennis Hayes. Nate informed Leslie that Dennis was a long-time customer who had several bed and breakfast establishments near The Jersey Shore and wanted to furnish all of them with Paradise Pillows' top of the line pillows, pillow cases and sheets. That was all she knew of Dennis Hayes.

Leslie checked the time again and decided she had ample time to relax in the Jacuzzi before meeting Dennis at three that afternoon. "First, I will unpack and hang up my business suit so it will look fresh; call room service for a bottle of Moscato and a cheese and cracker platter with grapes," she exhaled softly. "Yes, that is just what I need for now," as she quickly undressed and turned on the water for the Jacuzzi to fill up. She put on the soft white bath robe hanging up in the marbled, tiled bathroom and called room service. The room service attendant arrived very shortly with everything just as she ordered. The attendant entered her room and popped open the Moscato and poured her a drink.

"Ummmm," Thank you so much, as she sipped the ice cold Moscato, giving him a nice hefty tip which he gladly accepted.

"If you need anything else Ms. Stamford, please call," he said, as he exited the room.

Leslie quickly disrobed and settled in the hot Jacuzzi tub filled with bubbles and her drink. "How refreshing," she thought, as she finished her third class of wine and drifted off to sleep.

She was awakened suddenly from her unexpected nap feeling very cold. She was grateful for the now chilly water causing her to wake up. "Oh my goodness, what time is it?" she thought, as she jumped out of the tub and wrapped herself in a towel, shivering slightly. She quickly walked into the bedroom to look at the clock, still feeling a buzz from the wine she had consumed earlier. Whew, a sigh of relief she thought. It was now 2PM. Just enough time to get dressed and meet Dennis at the flowing fountain in the center of the lobby at 3PM.

****

Dennis Hayes arrived around 1PM dressed in a Stacey Adams' business suit. He immediately took his overnight bag to his room and returned to the lounge bar and had a few martinis to unwind. Dennis was a savvy business-minded 33 year old handsome man. He worked hard over the years and was now enjoying the benefit of all his hard work. He had purchased twelve colonial homes on The Jersey Shore Boulevard and converted them into Bed and Breakfast Suites. He was responsible for a staff of thirty seven full-time employees, three assigned to each suite and one maintenance man. They were an exceptional staff who excelled in creating the warm hospitable ambience for the many returning tourists who sought out Hayes Bed and Breakfast Suites. He was very proud of his staff and his accomplishments, considering where he had come from...the projects of Bedford Sty in Brooklyn, New York.

Reared by a single parent, his mother, Gloria had three children. Dennis was the baby boy who loved the attention of his two older sisters. Gloria worked two jobs and provided shelter for her family in the Projects of Bedford Sty. She was a hard worker and very focused on providing the very best for her children. She always would say, "hard work will pay off and it will get us out of the projects, but it takes everyone of us to do their part. We are family and family stick together, family work together, family reap together."

As soon as Dennis turned 16 years old, he took the role of providing for the family by doing odd jobs after school and the weekends to help provide for the family. After all the bills were paid, Dennis saved every dime he had left over. By the time he turned 22 years old, he purchased his first piece of real estate and began flipping properties.

They were indeed a close knit family who looked forward to Sundays. Sunday was church day and family time together. After church, the girls would help Gloria prepare a big meal that everyone enjoyed as they told stories of what had happened during the week. They wanted it to be really special because Gloria was not able to spend much time with them during the week because of her work schedule. Every opportunity, Gloria reminded them that they all were smart and could do and be anything they set their minds to. She was exceptionally proud that they were very obedient and respectful and that each of them had big goals and dreams. It gave Gloria great peace of mind when she would leave them to go to work. During the week, she worked as a Home Health Aide. She helped an older gentleman who suffered a stroke and was bed ridden. In the evenings, she cleaned office buildings to support her family.

Dennis' father left them when he was three years old. As Dennis grew older he saw the drug dealers, the pimps and the junkies. He loved the way the drug dealers and pimps dressed. He declared, "I will wear the best clothes one day, but I will be a legit businessman. His dream came true. When he turned 26, he purchased his mother her first home on the outskirts of New Jersey. She gave up cleaning the office buildings and focused on caring for the disabled. It was very rewarding for her to help others who could not help themselves.

Dennis' sisters, Sandy and Diane stayed with them until they graduated with their licenses as Registered Nurses. They both married and moved out, but he stayed. He felt he needed to be the man of the house and look after his momma. Gloria soon opened up her home to do private care. Finally she had her own business. Another answered prayer and dream come true. It all worked out well. There was plenty room in the five bedroom house. Dennis took the basement and converted it into his own man cave.

Dennis felt very relaxed after his second martini. He made small talk with the bartender and munched on fresh peanuts. Settling his thoughts about meeting with Teresa's assistant, his easy going personality suddenly changed to strictly business. He was austere when it came to business, but he began to feel awkward too because he could not remember Teresa' assistant's name. Was it a man or a woman? Should I call Nate to ask, he thought. No, I will just wait. We are to meet at the huge flowing fountain in the center of the hotel lobby at 3PM. Glancing at this watch it was now 2:30PM. Dennis motioned to the bartender, one more please as he quickly downed the Martini and left for his room to freshen up a bit. At least use some mouth wash, he concluded. Dennis never drank this much when he was going to do business, but he felt nervous for some reason, another martini will take off the edge he thought. Maybe it was because he did not know who he was meeting and had always worked with Nate or Teresa. Either way, I must get the best price possible of Paradise's top-of-the-line bedding apparel for my string of Bed and Breakfast Suites, he thought.

CHAPTER 13

Michael was excited. Tomorrow is Saturday and he will be getting back on the road to New York. He really hated to say good bye to Charlie. God had certainly taken Michael out of his comfort zone. All that he experienced had humbled him in such a way that his life was altered forever. Michael continued to long to see Teresa and Jamie. He wondered how it would be when they saw each other. "Would Teresa forgive me? Would she despise my very presence? Did she get married?"

Michael's thoughts were interrupted as he heard a car approaching. "Hey Charlie, we have a visitor," he yelled. Charlie slid out from underneath the truck, squinting trying to acclimate to the bright sun.

"Oh, Hi Pastor Jo," he said, wiping his hands on a soiled and greased rag. "What brings you out here today?" he said smiling showing his one tooth.

"Well, as I was praying this morning, I felt the Holy Spirit prompting me to come out here today to visit with you. Pastor Jo smiled at Michael and sensed Michael was the reason for this visit.

"Ahh, forgive me and my manners. Pastor Jo, this here is Mike. Mike this is my Pastor, Pastor Jo Robinson," smiling proudly.

"Well, it is really nice to meet you. Charlie has spoken very highly of you. I feel honored to meet you personally, Michael said shaking his hand.

"I am just about finished with the truck and it should be as good as new. I guess you will be leaving tomorrow. I can't keep you another day?" he said, teasing Michael.

Turning to Pastor Jo, Charlie said, "I got dinner cooking already and you are welcome to stay. It would be mighty nice to have a good Bible Study after dinner tonight. What'cha say?"

"That sounds mighty fine," said Pastor Jo. "I am looking forward to the fellowship."

Within a few hours, everyone was settled around the little table and enjoying the pot luck stew that consisted of all the leftovers from earlier in the week. Charlie added a cup of cornmeal to the well seasoned water to thicken the broth. It was hearty, tasty and filling…but nothing would fill their souls like what followed next.

Pastor Jo stood up and motioned Charlie and Michael to follow. As they stood, Pastor Jo bowed his head and began to pray. *"O Mighty God, we invoke your presence and I am reminded of your Word in Jeremiah 33:3, where you said, Call unto me and I will answer you and show you great and mighty things which thou know not."* He repeated it again, but this time it was more of a command to Charlie and Michael to call on Jesus. Just as they began to call on the name of Jesus, the Glory of God filled the little shack. It was an undeniable bright light that was brighter than the noon-day sun. Charlie's and Michael's legs buckled as they fell prostrate on the floor and were immediately in the presence of God, weeping uncontrollably. Pastor Jo remained standing and the Spirit of Prophesy came upon him. He kneeled beside Michael and placed his hand on his head. *"Thus saith the Lord, the Holy One of Israel, my son, this is your appointed time to know these things. Think it not strange that you desire to return to your past for it is I who has placed that desire in you. It is necessary before you move into the place I have for you that you release your past guilt and shame. For I have called you to go to the nations with the message of love and forgiveness. I am calling you to counsel the broken hearted and set the captive free and lead them to Me. Your assignment will begin a few days from now. You will soon meet my servant who will pour into you and thrust you forward and teach you many things. You will be filled with My Word, My Power and Holy Boldness! Your assignment and destiny is ordained by Me and I will lead you and guide you by the unction of My Spirit. Fear no man and speak the words that I will put in your mouth. The words I give you will bring hope and life to*

102

dead situations. For out of your belly will flow rivers of living water. Receive ye the Holy Ghost to do my will NOW saith the Lord of Hosts!"

Michael surrendered to the Holy Spirit of God and as he said yes to God, God filled him with the Spirit and he spoke in an unknown tongue. He cried and repented as he lay prostrate on the floor in the little shack, humbled, broken and changed forever. Suddenly Michael saw himself suspended in the air looking down at his body on the floor. He was immediately looking at an outline of the world spinning on its axle. He saw all the continents of the world. He saw himself dressed in clergy garments preaching in churches, tents, and opened fields as well as many different types of platforms to large and small audiences. He saw a large cross on top of a church with the name "Light of Love" that seemed to burn with fire. As suddenly as it happened, Michael was suddenly back into his body on the floor. Michael realized he had an out-of-body experience and God took him up in a vision to show him what was yet to come. He understood the prophecy, and the vision, but the words on the church steeple that burned with fire were yet the real mystery.

Charlie and Pastor Jo cried and praised God for Michael's encounter, although they could not see his out-of-body experience, but they saw the Shekinah Glory of God which filled the little shack in a thick smoky white cloud. They knew and understood his life would never be the same again. It was not by coincidence that his truck broke down and he had to stay there for over a week. It was all a part of God's plan for him to receive this divine impartation.

CHAPTER 14

Troy arrived at Teresa's apartment at 6PM sharp with two dozen fresh yellow roses, a large variety of Chinese food and a thin leather brief case. Teresa answered the door and cordially invited him in. Troy smiled with a big grin as he offered her the flowers and a light hug.

"Oh, they are beautiful Teresa said, but you didn't have to…"

Troy interrupted and said, "It is my pleasure to hand-deliver these beautiful flowers to a beautiful lady."

Teresa blushed as she motioned him into the kitchen with the food. "Please put them here on the table."

"Oh, Troy, you remember my son Jamie right?" Oh, yes of course he said confidently. Jamie you have grown quite a bit since I saw you last, reaching out to shake his hand.

"Yes. Ricky said, I am growing into a man now and I have to look out for Momma" he beamed.

Teresa smiled nervously and tried to change the subject. Troy gave her a quick wink and focused on Jamie. Troy smiled and nodded; yes, Ricky told you right. Maybe you and I can get together to do some big man stuff, whatcha say to that?"

Jamie smiled and shook his hand and quickly looked at the flowers on the table. "The flowers are pretty Momma," eyeing Troy as if he knew what he was up to. "You brought these here for my Momma?"

Well, yes, Jamie. When I saw how beautiful these flowers were, I thought of your mother and how beautiful she is and thought she deserved them. Don't you think they are beautiful like your Momma?"

Jamie shook his head in agreement.

"And, I brought Chinese food too. You like Chinese food, right?"

"Yes, Mr. Kennedy. Thank you very much. Momma, can we eat now?" Troy quickly interrupted, "Jamie, I know you are calling me Mr. Kennedy to show me respect because I am an adult. Your mother is teaching you to be respectful; but, if it is okay with you and your mother, I would like you to call me Troy. It makes me feel like I am your big brother and a good friend. Is that okay with everyone?"

Jamie and Teresa smiled and shook their heads in agreement. Teresa could not help but feel very comfortable, and the conversation seemed to just flow; it did not feel forced at all. It seemed natural.

Soon everyone had eaten and the kitchen was cleaned. Jamie excused himself to take his shower and Teresa and Troy returned to her cozy living room.

Troy quickly took out the brochures of the country club. The bright and colorful pictures advertising the country club were amazing! Teresa was awestruck! There was miniature golf, rock climbing, tennis courts, horseback riding, skating, swimming, dancing, spas, fishing, row boating, movie theaters, elegant dining areas and lots of things to do all day and all night. It looked like a small paradise with all sorts of entertainment for all ages. So many things to do and it all looked like fun and relaxation. Troy smiled as he watched Teresa's eyes widen with excitement.

"Well, I know you were looking for someplace to get away for a week or so and I actually think this would be a perfect fit for all of us. It will be great and lots of fun and it's only an hour away. What do you think Teresa?"

"This looks like a yes, but I would like you to leave the brochures. I will let you know tomorrow? I need to check out the expenditures."

"Oh, no" Troy said, "you and Jamie will be my guest, and I will take care of all the expenses."

"Absolutely not," Teresa said firmly and if you insist this will definitely be a deal breaker. I must pay my own way. I do appreciate your offer, but we must be clear as to what is expected of each other. If I should go, we are strictly friends. You will sleep in your own room and Jamie and I will sleep in ours. We are not boyfriend/girlfriend. We are not dating, we are just friends. We are…"

"Hey, hey, hey, it is okay," he said interrupting. "I get it. It's okay Teresa. Please don't worry about me being anything other than your friend and a perfect gentleman." Smiling, he moved over to shake her hand as if to imply a truce.

Teresa relaxed and gave out a sigh of relief. "I just don't want to have any misunderstanding between us, that's all."

"No problem, my friend. Would you like to leave Sunday or Monday? I know it would be better if we arrive late Sunday afternoon, and be all settled in for Monday's activities."

"Sunday sounds fine. But I will confirm everything with you tomorrow. Leaving on Sunday will give me plenty of time to get our things packed." Teresa was actually feeling excited but did not want it to show. It was already too late. Troy knew she was excited and he was looking forward to getting as close as possible to Teresa and Jamie on this mini vacation.

CHAPTER 15

Judge Harris could hardly restrain himself. He got out of his car singing and skipping to his house as if he had just won the lottery. He rushed into his house and put the ice cream in the freezer. He had totally forgotten it and it had become soft. Momma King had messed him up. His inner soul had been awakening. He quickly flopped into his Lazy Boy chair with his feet up and picked up the phone and dialed Momma King's number.

"Hello?" Momma King said smiling, knowing it was Judge Harris.

"Hello Joni. It's me, Les Harris. I am happy to hear your voice again. Is this a good time for you?"

"Yes, yes, of course. I am really glad you called."

Momma King and Judge Les Harris laughed and giggled like high school sweethearts for the next three hours. They had talked way past their regular bed time. They discussed many things, their likes and dislikes, their relationship with God, and their deceased spouses and why neither had children. They both admitted that it was not a deliberate plan to not have children; it just worked out that way. She did share with Les her special relationship and bond with Teresa and Jamie. They discussed the

Bible and their faith in God as believers. They did not realize just how much they had in common. They thanked God for allowing their paths to cross.

She learned that Judge Harris was also a devout Christian who held the position of a deacon at his church every Sunday, but seemed to be locked into religious traditions. She knew in time she could show him the difference of being religious and having a personal relation with Jesus. She was delighted to know he had strong moral values, deep convictions and loved Jesus.

Les learned that Joni was a Bible Teacher at her church and would be ministering on the gifts of the Holy Spirit next week. He knew it was going to be an awesome experience. Just listening to her expound on the Word had made him thirsty to know more. He was elated and was looking forward to attending every night with her.

He belonged to a denomination which did not teach on the gifts of God. He often wanted to know more about the Power of God but the pastor never taught on it, or anyone else. He read his bible faithfully and came to realize that there was much more than what his church was teaching. His steadfastness and faithfulness kept him bound to the church he was reared in. He never even thought about visiting any other church until now. He thanked God that he would finally get to venture out from his denomination and learn more. He was especially pleased that he could go and support Joni and still not miss any of his obligations at his own church. She would start teaching each night for nine nights beginning on Sunday.

Judge Harris suggested he come over to her house after church for the dinner she promised him, and they could go to church together that evening. She agreed, even though she really wanted to spend quiet time with God before going to church to teach. "Oh well," she thought, "I can spend all day Saturday preparing my notes. I will fast and pray on Saturday seeking God's face for a fresh anointing to teach His Word on Sunday. God is always faithful. He will see me through as always."

They prayed for each other and invited the presence of God into their newly found friendship before hanging up. They both felt free and happy as they fell off to sleep. Judge Harris was so comfortable he never went to bed; he drifted off with his legs up in his Lazy Boy, smiling at the thought of finally meeting Ms. Joni King. "Thank you Jesus! She is truly a gift from God...perfect in every way!"

CHAPTER 16

Leslie realized she had had too much to drink and was feeling a little woozy. She stepped out of the hotel room fully dressed in her linen coral suit and designer pumps, looking amazingly beautiful in spite of her mental state of drunkenness. She had sprayed on a little extra of her favorite scent, Casmir in an attempt to conceal the odor of alcohol. I have to be down in the lobby by the fountain in a few minutes; it is too late for some strong black coffee now. Oh well, Dennis Hayes does not know me and he will not know that I had too much to drink, she reasoned with herself. I just have to hold it together to get this deal done for Nate, and then I am going back to my room and sleep the rest of the night, she thought.

Leslie stepped in the elevator and pushed the button for the lobby. The elevator stopped on the 6th floor. A young couple stepped in and quickly pushed the button for the lobby as well. They were so enthralled with each other they did not notice Leslie holding tightly to the rail. The stopping motion of the elevation made her feel nauseous. Finally the door opened at the lobby level. Leslie slowly stepped out, trying to keep her composure. She could see the fountain but no one seemed to be there waiting for her. She decided to make a quick stop in the ladies room just in case. Grateful for the lounge chair in the room, she took a seat and waited until the nauseous feeling subsided.

Glancing at her watch, she realized it was 3:02PM. She quickly rose from the chair and peeked out. There was a man standing looking opposite her direction. She could not see his face, just the fact that he was about 6'2" with a muscular build, in a dark brown suit. Oh, that must be Dennis Hayes, she thought. Taking another quick look in the mirror, she headed toward the fountain. Dennis turned and looked directly at her as she approached. "Oh my goodness," he muttered to himself. "Is this Teresa's assistant?" Suddenly remembering he had forgotten her name he could not remove his eyes from her. He knew at that moment this was the reason he was still a single man...waiting for her. He knew that she could not be married and she had to be his wife. Feeling the deep gaze, Leslie's legs begin to tremble as she too, looked upon the most handsome man she had ever seen. Ricky Clay could not even compete with him. In addition to her feeling nauseous, now she could not breathe. *"O God If You are really real, please don't let me trip, faint or throw up." Please God, not now!"*

Without missing a beat, Dennis walked towards Leslie with his hand extended; you must be Teresa's assistant, he said, revealing pearly white teeth behind a thick heavy black mustache. His light colored hazel eyes bore deep into her soul and he knew without a doubt, "this little lady here is my soul mate, my wife forever."

"Ah, yes, Leslie Stamford here and you must be Dennis Hayes," as she placed her hand in his. They gazed tongue-tied at each other for several seconds. Both feeling overwhelmed with unusual joy and happiness.

"It is truly my pleasure to meet you Leslie. Please, before getting down to business, would you like to have dinner in the lounge upstairs?"

"Yes, I think that would be great," nodding her head. Food was exactly what she needed along with a strong cup of black coffee, she thought.

Dinner, conversation, and this new friendship was the beginning of pure ecstasy for both. They wasted no time in getting acquainted. It was love at first sight.

They looked like the perfect couple in the eyes of everyone who served them. The coral suit Leslie wore looked lovely with the dark brown suit Dennis had on even in the picture they took together that evening. They decided they would spend the evening enjoying each other's company and do "business" the next day. After dinner, they had several more drinks before leaving the lounge. It was about 2AM, when Dennis escorted Leslie to her room and said good night. They both were buzzed from the liquor they had consumed and the enchantment of each other.

"I will see you first thing tomorrow morning so we can finish up our business. May I give you a goodnight hug?" he suggested.

"Yes, yes, of course," she said blushing at the secret thought she had as she opened the door to her room. She did not want him to go, now or ever. They hugged each other very passionately. Both were grateful another couple stepped out of the elevator, glaring at them with suspicion. Leslie and Dennis let go of each other. Between the alcohol and their emotional state, she did not trust her vulnerability. She quickly stepped into her room and said, "I'll see you tomorrow," closing the door. "It was only a hug, but it could have easily turned into something on a totally different level," she thought breathing heavily.

CHAPTER 17

Michael was a changed man with a new heart and a new outlook on life. He woke up excited. He knew he finally had a purpose in life and looked forward to God having complete control of his every step. God promised to send him to the nations. He was so excited. He wondered how he was going to tell Teresa and Jamie. He thought how he was going to persuade them to come with him. He finally realized his thinking was "his" way of thinking... not God's way. He remembered it was God who had the plan for "*his*" life and not he himself, and God knows exactly how to do everything.

He said his good bye to Charlie late Saturday afternoon. He vowed to write as soon as he got settled. Charlie actually cried as he hugged Michael and called him his "brother." It was an amazing week for both. Michael embraced Charlie as well, and placed a large sum of money in his hand. "My brother and friend, the Word of God says a servant or a laborer is worthy of his hire. I hired you to fix my truck and you did that plus!! So please accept this as my way of saying thank you for everything. And please be sure to give your pastor a love offering for me. Okay?" Charlie had not seen that amount of money ever at one time. He was speechless!

"Thank you so much my friend and my brother in Christ. I am really sad to see you go."

"Yes, Charlie, my friend, my brother in Christ, thank you for your kind and gracious hospitality. I will write to you as soon as I get settled wherever God is leading me." Michael climbed into his truck and drove down the beaten path. Even the old dog came out from under the shade tree wagging his tail as if to say good bye.

****

Michael was all the more anxious to get to New York to see Teresa and his son, Jamie. He figured he would arrive late Sunday afternoon or early evening. He spent a lot of time thinking about Teresa and Jamie, and praising God.

Exhausted, sleepy and hungry, Michael decided to stop in Georgia and get a good meal and a good night's rest. "With another fourteen hours to go, I will be in New York around 5 or 6PM on Sunday evening. My first stop will be at Teresa's apartment. Well, it has been almost 9 years, what if she moved? What will I do to find her? Wherever she and Jamie are, I am determined to find them and make things right, no matter what," he thought.

"Wow, this has truly been a journey and it's just the beginning, he said, choking back tears. It will be a complete circle returning back to New York." Overwhelmed with the presence of God, He began rejoicing and proclaiming out loud, "God really does love me in spite of what I have done. He even has a plan for my life. Thank you Jesus! Thank you Father God! Thank you Holy Spirit." He sat in his truck for a few minutes basking in the presence of Almighty God before checking into the hotel.

After getting his room key, Michael decided to eat a wonderful home cooked meal. Eating something familiar was definitely on the menu. He was humbled and grateful thinking of Charlie's dinner of Muskrat and Swamp Cabbage versus this menu he had to choose from.

"Okay," he said, as the waitress approached. "I will have fried chicken, mashed potatoes with brown gravy, fresh string beans and a piece of the honey buttered cornbread with a large sweet iced tea."

"Sure thang sir" replied the waitress, writing on her pad. "I will be back shortly."

"Oh, and you can bring the desert as well...a bowl of peach cobbler." He yelled as an afterthought.

Dinner was very filling and satisfying. Afterwards, he went to his room and took a long hot shower. He debated with himself as to whether to shave his full beard he managed to grow while staying with Charlie.

"No, I think I like it," after looking at himself for a while. "Yes, I think I will keep it. It is part of the new me," he declared. He prayed to God for Teresa and Jamie to welcome the "new" Michael, and to forgive him.

"Oh well, I will see them tomorrow, Sunday evening. Will they be in church? Did they even go to church?" He was nervous and excited about seeing them; but, his exhaustion won out. He remembered thanking God for the comfort of the large queen-sized bed and his tummy which was full of his favorite foods before drifting off to sleep.

CHAPTER 18

Judge Harris arrived at Momma King's house early Sunday afternoon. They enjoyed the dinner she prepared and laughed and talked like old friends. Soon it was time to leave to go to church. Momma King was excited to be teaching tonight on one of the nine gifts of the Holy Spirit. Judge Harris was equally excited. Momma King gave him the recording machine with some blank tapes, stating she promised Teresa and Jamie, that she would record the teaching for them. "They just left this afternoon to take a week's vacation. I hope they will have a good time. She really needs some peace of mind. You remember Troy Kennedy, who was her attorney, right?"

"Of course, no, wait a minute. They went on vacation together?" Before Momma King could answer him, he said smiling, "I knew it! I knew it! I thought he had a special interest in her when he showed up in my courtroom pleading her case because she was late for her appointment earlier in the week. I think it is a beautiful thing to find someone to love and spend the rest of your life with. He made the statement and the way he looked at her, she knew he was not only talking about Teresa and Troy, but "them" as well.

They arrived at the church about a half hour before the evening service started. Mother King, (as she was known at church), was proud to introduce everyone to Judge Harris. Many of them raised their eyebrows, curious to know who this handsome man was with Mother King, while others already knew him as Judge Harris. Pastor Sherman welcomed him with open arms. He too, was just as surprised and curious as the rest of the congregation, as to what type of friendship it really was. He had known Judge Harris and Mother King for many years, but did not know they actually knew each other. Pastor Sherman even met with Judge Harris when Teresa was arrested and gave him a personal character reference for her, but he never mentioned he knew Mother King. "Oh well, If they are a couple then I am happy for them both," he said to himself, dismissing it. He knew him to be a good and fair judge. Pastor Sherman came to his courtroom from time to time when some of his parishioners got into some trouble.

Momma King was grateful that Pastor Sherman proudly showed Judge Harris around the edifice. Judge Harris was very impressed and felt honored to be there. After a full tour of the church, Pastor Sherman offered him a seat in the front row with the deacons. Momma King excused herself to spend a few minutes with the Lord before she began to teach. He nodded and touched her hand briefly to show support and affection. She smiled shyly and quickly made her way up to the podium and took her designated seat.

Pastor Sherman took the microphone and welcomed everyone to the first night of learning about the gifts of God. Just then the door opened and a tall man who seemed to be in his early thirties walked in. He had a bewildered look in his eyes, and his facial expressions were concealed by the thick moustache and heavy black beard. He wore a black cowboy hat (which he quickly removed) and a light tan colored cashmere sport jacket; a green plaid shirt and black pants with pointed toed cowboy boots. He was definitely a first time visitor to Light of Love Ministries. His style of dressing confirmed he was not from the area. The Usher welcomed him and offered him a seat up front, but he hastily took a seat in the back. Pastor Sherman and the stranger's eyes met. They both smiled faintly, and then the Spirit of God spoke to Pastor Sherman, *"I have sent him to you. Prepare him for the journey that is ahead of him."* Overwhelmed by the Spirit of God, Pastor Sherman promptly introduced the woman of God, Mother Joni King and took his seat.

Mother King took her place at the podium and was pleased to see the church almost as full as it was on Sunday morning. She noticed the stranger as well. There was something about him that seemed familiar in some way. She quickly dismissed the thought and got refocused on teaching God's Word.

"Dearly beloved, I stand before you this evening, humbled and honored to teach on one of the nine gifts of the Holy Spirit. I have all of my notes here to teach on Wisdom, but the Lord, whom I trust and will obey has instructed me to teach on the gift of miracles, the miraculous power of miracles.

Judge Harris promptly pushed the record button. He was proud to play such a small, but significant role for her. Mother King spoke under the anointing and instructions of the Holy Spirit for one hour with great confidence and power. "Let's first define a miracle and I would like to show a few examples you can find in your Bible," she said.

"A miracle is an act of the Holy Spirit that defies the law of nature. When there is no means of natural provision, God is able to provide through the working of miracles. There are Christians who do not believe that God works miracles today, but I stand before you tonight to say why should it be strange for God to work miracles today, especially when they are seen throughout the scriptures. For example, in Acts 9:36-42, we find Peter, one of Jesus' disciples raising the dead and a few chapters later in Acts 12:3-19, we find Peter locked up in jail, and the power of prayer invoked an angel of God to deliver him from his prison cell! The chains fell off him and he was able to walk past the guards unseen."

"That's a Miracle!" Mother King proclaimed, shouting "Halleluiah." Many echoed her shouting, Halleluiah and amen as well. Mother King continued.

"The Angel of God even caused the iron gates to open by itself and Peter walked out a free man. It is my desire to show you tonight that God still performs miracles and has given us the same ability through faith and belief. Some miracles are manifested through fasting and prayer and some have the gift of miracles which can be performed by the laying on of hands and speaking with authority the Word of God by faith in the name of Jesus Christ, the Son of the living God. Please get your pen and paper out; I will explain the difference between a miracle and the gift of miracles. Miracles happen every day. "There are many examples in the Bible of miracles, " she continued.

"In Exodus chapter 14:21-22, when God parted the Red Sea to allow the Israelites to cross, that was a miracle. Another example is to be translated; (to suddenly be in another place or another city instantly). Genesis 5:24 reminds us of Enoch, who never died; he was translated from earth to heaven. That's a miracle, and is scientifically unexplainable.

A supernatural occurrence is like when the Kingdom of God came to the earth to live in a physical clay vessel. A vessel that was made of dirt until He breathed life into the earthly clay and it became a living soul. That's the miraculous power of God! Scientifically you can't explain it, but it is real. Your

124

salvation is a miracle. When you invited Jesus into your heart to be Lord over your life, something happened on the inside of you. You can't see it, you can't touch it, but you know it is there and it is real because it changed the sin-infested heart to a heart that no longer desires to sin, but to live holy. God is a Holy God. He said, "Be Holy for I am Holy."

"This teaching is to define a miracle. Tomorrow we will talk about the Gift of Miracles, which is given to some believers today. Tonight we have laid the foundation of miracles," she continued in her conclusion. "Yes, to those who have been born-again, it is a miracle because you were once an enemy of God, bound and blind to sin. Jesus shed his precious blood that cleansed your sin in-festered soul and revealed himself to you. He took away the old stony heart and gave you a heart of flesh. A heart that is sensitive to God and his ways. This, my brothers and sisters is the greatest miracle of all... our salvation! If there is anyone here tonight who wants to experience the miracle of salvation, please come to the altar now so we may pray with you to receive Jesus as the Lord of your life".

Mother King marveled at what came out of her mouth. She had no idea that those scriptures were hidden down in her spirit. They were scriptures in the Bible that she knew were there, but she did not know that she knew exactly where they were written. As she stood teaching, she realized the words she spoke were not her own. That in itself, was a miracle! The

125

message filled the appetite of every hungry parishioner, including Pastor Sherman, Judge Harris, herself and the stranger! Judge Harris had joy unspeakable. He had never heard a message that filled him with so much hope and expectancy. I can really believe God for miracles, he thought. He loved the teaching.

God used Mother King to teach in such a fashion the scriptures became alive to the listeners. The stories and examples of the miracle working power of the Holy Spirit seemed to rest upon everyone. Several people came to the altar and gave their lives to Jesus and receive salvation. Three ministers came forward to lead them in the prayer of salvation.

Pastor Sherman returned to the podium. He beamed with pride at the exegetical she delivered.

"What an awesome teaching from Mother King. The only thing I can add to that is I am proud to say I am her pastor!

Everyone laughed and gave Mother King a round of applause.

"Please remember to join us tomorrow night, same time for more teaching on the gifts of God." He gave the benediction and encouraged everyone to greet each other. The stranger with the large cowboy hat began to make his way towards the front of the church. Many stopped to greet and welcome him along the way. He smiled and acknowledged the love, but stayed focused on moving forward, his eyes were fixed on Mother King. Pastor Sherman's eyes were fixed on him.

Judge Harris joined Mother King congratulating her and reassuring her that he had taped the entire teaching for Teresa. She smiled and thanked him. The stranger stepped in front of her, smiling, with his hand extended. Judge Harris stayed close by her side.

"Hi Mrs. King. It is nice to see you again. My soul was truly blessed, and I learned so much!"

Mother King stared at him trying to remember him. Smiling gracefully, she finally spoke. Thank you so much, and you do look very familiar but I am sorry, I ...

Interrupting her, Oh, I am Michael Hayden, Jamie's father.

"Well! Well! Well!" Mother King exclaimed. "Wow, it has been nine years since I saw you."

"Yes, m'am it has been. I went to see Teresa and Jamie, but the neighbor told me they just left earlier today on a week's vacation.

"Yes, you are right. They are away now, and they're going to be surprised to see you here."

"Mrs. King, It was a miracle that I am here tonight. Just as you were teaching, an unexplained occurrence happened to me. After I left Teresa's apartment, the Spirit of God led me here. I did not know where I was going until I saw the sign that was inflamed in fire saying Light and Love. I saw the same words in flames in a vision a few days ago, but I did not know it was a church. So, here I am.

"Wow, that is a miracle indeed. God is truly amazing," she confirmed.

"Mrs. King I was wondering if it is not too much to ask if I could come by maybe tomorrow to talk a bit since they are going to be away for a week. I would love to know as much as I can about Jamie and Teresa before I see them face to face. I am nervous about it but I just want to make things right. I am saved now and God has blessed me and I want to take care of mine," Michael blurted.

"Well now hold on, I am very happy you are saved now and God has really blessed you, but with all due respect, I don't think it would be wise to have you over while they are on vacation. The truth of the matter is that I think you need to speak to them directly before getting an inside scoop from me about what has happened with them or to them the past nine years. Please don't be offended, but I want to be fair to everyone involved here. Once you have spoken to them and you ALL decide you would like to come to my house then you are more than welcome, but not until then."

Judge Harris stepped in closer, holding Mother King by the arm. "Is everything okay?" he asked.

"Oh yes, Michael Hayden meet Les Harris. Michael is Jamie's father who has been absent for the past nine years."

They shook hands. She tried to smile.

"Oops, I am sorry. I did not mean for that to sound condescending or judgmental. Really, it was just awkward trying to make the introduction. I am very happy that you are here. It is very obvious that God definitely has a plan for your life here at Light of Love Ministries. Let me introduce you to my pastor."

She motioned Pastor Sherman over. He had been watching the stranger from afar. He came right over.

"Pastor Sherman, meet Michael Hayden. He used to live here," making sure she did not make the same mistake again. Pastor Sherman shook his hand and said, "Yes, God told me He had directed you here for an impartation." Michael's eyes widened with excitement. "Really? What's that?"

"Let's talk tomorrow. Where are you from?"

"Austin, Texas."

"Do you have a place to stay?"

"Actually, No Sir, but I was planning to get a hotel room someplace nearby."

"No, you can stay here. This is the first part of the impartation... hospitality. We have a few beautiful guest quarters. No Chefs are on the premises though, Pastor Sherman teased. But you can order in and there are delivery services in the area available as well. There is literature in the room. Come on. Let me show you."

CHAPTER 19

Troy arrived at Teresa's around 5PM on Sunday evening to start their week-long vacation. Teresa was on the phone with Momma King.

"Momma King, please don't forget to record the teaching on the Gifts of the Holy Spirit for me and Jamie. I gotta run now, Troy just came to pick us up. Keep us in prayer okay?"

"I sure will. Have a wonderful time and when you come back I have some good news to share with you. I have met someone who is going to go with me tonight to the teaching."

"Okay" she said. It never once entered her mind that Momma King was talking about a man she may be interested in. It was normal for Momma King to bring people to church with her.

They all were excited as they headed for The Harlem Attorney Country Club to get away from the hustle and bustle of their norm. Troy carefully added their luggage in the back of his Range Rover. Jamie quickly became attached to Troy and he genuinely enjoyed lavishing Teresa and Jamie with lots of affection and attention. It was a perfect week of healing and letting down barriers for everyone.

They did everything together. They laughed, they held hands while they skated, enjoyed deep interesting conversations, and they shared their faith and belief in God. Teresa shared her issues about the abandonment of her mother and Michael. She never talked about Ricky; but she did share some of her fears, insecurities and trust issues. Troy never pushed, and shared his hurt and disappointments in the last relationship he was in as well. They had a very open and honest connection and dialogue; they seemed to balance each other nicely. Jamie seemed to know exactly when to exit the conversation.

"Momma, I am going to go play with Will and David," the two brothers who were there on vacation as well. He was always nearby, but sometimes doing other things with his new friends, giving his momma and Troy some "alone time."

She began to examine herself and decided she had to bring some things to an end ... starting with Ricky's letters. She debated whether she should read them or just burn them. She was afraid that if she read them, he would somehow convince her to wait for him with promises of marriage. She was afraid he would still be able to manipulate her, even from jail. It suddenly dawned on her that she had to be strong and face her fears and refuse to allow him to control and manipulate her. After all, surely he could not expect me to wait for him to get out of jail. He was sentenced to 15 years to life.

She still loved him, but after this time with Troy she saw that it was possible to love again; to heal and embrace something new. She moved on from the heartbreak of Michael walking out on her and Jamie when he was born, when she met Ricky Clay. Now here with Troy, he had made her laugh and filled her with hope and the possibility of what life could be for her and Jamie. He encouraged her to pursue her dreams; he made everything seem like it was possible, even her idea of returning to school to become a Social Worker. So many things changed. Teresa felt strong and confident. She realized that Troy was an asset to her life as well as Jamie's. This was just what the doctor ordered, real rest and relaxation with a real gentleman. She really felt great about the vacation and Troy's friendship. She thought of Momma King telling her not to rule him out because of his age. She laughed out loud.

Troy asked "what's so funny?"

"Oh, it was nothing. Just my own private thoughts, and you are not allowed there," she teased. Teresa had a lot of private thoughts, especially on the ride back home. She was in deep thought. Could Troy be the one for her? It has only been a week, but she felt refreshed and ready to start anew. She prayed the same for Jamie. He and Troy really seemed to bond when they went fishing and rock climbing together. She thought of Momma King and wondered how the teachings were on the nine gifts of the Holy Spirit. She wondered if Momma King remembered to record the teachings for her. She wondered if there were answers in the teaching concerning her and Troy. Jamie and I will be able to get to the last two nights of the teachings, and maybe Troy would like to come as well. We will be home in less than an hour and I can't wait to see Momma King to tell her everything.

Troy tried hard to get her to talk about what was on her mind. She said, "maybe one day, but for now, they are my own little private thoughts." The bona fide truth was she did not want the vacation to end. She really liked being with Troy. He made her feel smart, and pretty, and showed great interest in her and her opinion about everything that mattered. He seemed to genuinely care about her and Jamie, and was the perfect gentleman.

They soon pulled up in front of Teresa's apartment. It was late Sunday evening. Troy and Jamie quickly carried in their luggage. Teresa did not want him to leave, so she asked him if he would like to have a cup of coffee. Troy refused the coffee because it was so late, but he said instead, "how about a cup of hot chocolate?"

Yes, I do have hot chocolate. It comes with marshmallows."

She surprised herself as she flirted a bit.

"Are you okay with that?"

"Sure that will be great if you will have a cup with me."

"Absolutely, I will get it ready and check on Jamie. He has school tomorrow and I have to take him. I think I will take the day off as well. I have some things I have to attend to. I am sure Nate will be okay with that. I will call him tomorrow morning."

Teresa noticed her phone was flashing, indicating she had several messages. Oh well, it can wait for now. She resumed her conversation with Troy.

"The Spring Recess went by fast. Can you believe it? A whole week we spent together and I must admit, I really had a nice time Troy." Teresa suddenly realized she was talking non-stop. Pausing just for a moment, feeling slightly aroused, she said, "Thank you Troy so much for inviting us."

Troy was feeling the moment as well and stepped in closer to her. "It was my pleasure. Looking into her eyes, *everything* was my pleasure" he repeated, as he pulled her close to him. Teresa froze and closed her eyes bracing herself for the kiss she thought was coming, but instead he gave her the most meaningful hug she had ever experienced. It was amazing; Teresa experienced goose bumps all over. "How could that be," she thought. Troy sensed something magnificent take place at that very moment too. God was in that hug for sure. "I think it is time to say Goodnight," he suggested. "Thanks for the hot chocolate and a wonderful vacation with a very beautiful woman and my new little buddy, Jamie. Give him a hug for me. I will call you tomorrow if that is okay?"

"Yes, of course, and thank you again. Good night Troy."

"Good night, Teresa."

CHAPTER 20

Teresa had a hard time unwinding that evening. She decided she would resolve some things that troubled her. She tucked Jamie in bed and returned to her bedroom. She pulled out all of Ricky's letters and debated with herself if she should read them or just toss them all? After several minutes of prayer, she decided she would read them. She was happy she had put them in numerical order previously, just in case this day did come when she was strong enough to read them. "Well tonight was the night," she thought, opening the first letter:

My Dearest Teresa,

I am sorry I hurt you and Jamie. I know you are angry with me right now and you have every right to be. I deserved that open-handed slap to my head and so much more. I never wanted to hurt you or reveal to you what I was really doing in the warehouse. I am sorry for my selfish actions and I never meant to pull you into my wicked schemes. I repented to God and I need to know that you have forgiven me too. I also wanted to say thank you for not pressing charges against me for kidnapping you. I really thought you had taken the money. It was a few million dollars that I was going to split with the BOYS. With my share, my intentions were to spend the rest of my life with you and Jamie and to relocate. But, when my friends came and I could not produce the money, I feared that they might try to harm you and Jamie and not believe me when I told them I did not have the money. While, I was locked-up in county jail, I realized the police set me up and took the money from my car. Forgive me because I really thought you took it. How could I have been so stupid and blind? You could never do such a thing.

Teresa, I opened an account in the total amount of $10,000.00 for you and Jamie. Please go to Compton Trust and get your money. Talk to Mr. Wenzel, the bank manager. He knows all about you and Jamie. I truly love you Teresa. I must admit, I was using you and Nate in the beginning to hide my illegal activities, but somewhere along the line, I truly did fall in love with you. When I realized how much I really loved you it was too late to stop my wrong doings. I was too far in and others were counting on me to deliver. Again, Teresa, I am very sorry.

I have spent many nights crying out to God and asking him for one more chance to make things right with you and Jamie. I know I can't ever make things right because of what has happened; I pray that I get the opportunity one day to show you and Jamie that I love you both. My heart's desire now is to live a holy and honorable life in God's sight. He has taken away my arrogance, pride and self destructive gangster-style behavior. I really see the light now, but I guess it is too late. I still have hope, and I have added your name to my visitor and correspondence list in hopes that you will come see me or write me. I pray you can forgive me, and that you still love me. Please tell Jamie that I have done something very bad and I have to spend time away to make it right, and I am sorry I disappointed him. I love you both always. Ricky Clay.

Teresa was overwhelmed. She decided she would not read anymore for now. Her heart hurt. She missed Ricky and determined to read every letter, and when finished she would move on with her life. She willed herself to stop crying and decided she would pray for strength. *"Oh, God please heal my broken heart and help me to move on with a fresh and new outlook on life. Please give me the strength to finish reading all of these letters and when I am finished, help me to be finished with Ricky as well. Thank you Jesus. Amen."* She crawled under the covers and in spite of her heartache, was soon fast asleep.

CHAPTER 21

Leslie had no other choice but to wear her only change of clothes; a pair of blue jeans with a red Paradise Pillows long sleeve tee shirt and her flat driving shoes. She decided she would check out of the hotel and make the hour drive back after lunch. The snugly fitting jeans and shirt tucked in with a brown leather belt accented her tiny waistline and curvy figure.

Dennis was enthralled. "She is stunning," he declared as he watched her from across the room. He stood up so she could see him. She smiled and gave a slight wave. He wore a yellow shirt with green Dockers and brown loafers. Leslie quickly glanced him over as well. "Not bad, not bad at all, she thought. "Heck, he is fine as sweet mellow wine, laughing at her corny rhyme as she joined him. "Good morning Leslie. You look beautiful," giving her a slight hug, "and you smell amazing!"

"Thanks Dennis, you look like a real champ yourself," she said shyly.

It was almost noon and they enjoyed a light brunch and decided to finally wrap up the business. Dennis was no longer worried about getting a good deal for the bed linen he was to purchase for his Bed and Breakfast Suites. It was no longer a priority. Whatever price Leslie quoted would be fine. He was more interested in thinking of a way to convince her to stay another night. They quickly handled the business at hand. Dennis accepted whatever price Leslie quoted and handed her a check for the full amount. They put away their business paraphernalia and focused on each other. Dennis broke the stare.

"Leslie, listen, I have something I want to say to you." Leslie leaned in closer, recognizing the seriousness in his voice. "I am 33 years old and single by choice. I was happy to stay that way because I am a man who knows exactly what he wants. Now, I know this may be a bit much to grasp so soon, but I always promised myself I would not settle for anything less than what I always dreamed of. Leslie, I know it has only been forty-eight hours since we met, but from the first time I saw you walking toward me you have been the center of my thoughts. Now with that being said, I would like to show you something today. Could you stay here another night and take a ride with me? I will take care of all the expense of course."

"Uh, awwh, I don't know what to say," Leslie whimpered.

"Just say yes, please Leslie, just say yes, I know you were planning to check out today, but you don't have to be back to work until Monday right?"

"Uh yes, but…"

"Please let's spend the rest of today together. I want to show you something. I know I am asking a lot and you don't really know me, but will you trust me to take a ride with me? Where I want to take you is about forty-five minutes away."

Leslie hesitated. "I guess there is not enough time to say let me think about it right?" She teased. "Are we leaving right now?"

"Yes, thank you Leslie."

"Okay, let me run to my room to get my purse and put these receipts in the room."

"Okay, I will meet you at the fountain after I take care of my bill and pay another night for you okay?"

"Yes, thank you," she yelled back.

"Hopefully, you will not be coming back here to stay tonight anyway," he thought to himself, "maybe I can talk her into staying at one of my bed and breakfast suites in Jersey tonight."

Leslie was a little fearful, but at the same time feeling daring and beautiful. I must not be so stupid that I don't tell somebody, she cautioned herself. When I get to my room, I will call Teresa. She really did not know anyone else to call, but thought it was smart to tell someone who she was with. Teresa was not at home, so she left a message on her voice mail. "Am I so desperate that I am leaving this hotel going only God knows where with a man that I hardly know? Well he is not a complete

142

stranger; he has been dealing with Teresa, Nate and Paradise Pillows for years. They know him," she said, trying to convince herself.

Suddenly, she reflected on Teresa and Ricky and how they seemed to be so much in love, but look what he did to her. He even kidnapped her and Jamie. Fear suddenly gripped her heart again. Leslie quickly dismissed it and continued to tell herself, he is different. He is not a criminal. He is gorgeous, successful and interested in me, she smiled.

She made her way to the fountain. There he was. He held two roses he obviously purchased at the hotel's gift shop. He smiled and took Leslie by her hand.

"Here's a yellow one for our new friendship and the red for the love that I know will never end. Do you believe in love at first sight?"

Leslie again was taken back. "He is moving a bit too fast," she thought. As if he was reading her thoughts, he said, "I know this may seem like I am moving too fast and I don't want to run you away, but I want you to know I meant what I said. I have waited a long time for that "special lady" and with everything in me…I feel and know I have found her."

I definitely believe in love at first sight, she thought, but I can't let him know I am head over heels too. I can't appear to be vulnerable and desperate.

Leslie looked into his eyes. "Do I have a say in the matter?"

"Okay, that's fair," He smiled. "You definitely have a say about how you feel, but don't say anything until tomorrow okay?"

"Oh okay, thanks, I will let you know." She smiled as she sniffed the roses.

Leslie loved the ride in Dennis's black convertible Corvette. She loved the attention and the conversation. It was deep, intimate and revealing. They learned so much about each other. It felt right and good to both of them.

Soon they pulled up in front of a large colonial home. Leslie's eyes widened as she took in this breath-taking home. It looked like a mansion. The navy blue awning bore the name Hayes Bed and Breakfast. The spotless white swinging love seat on the huge wrap-around porch looked very inviting. The array of flowers was lined symmetrically around the porch in many shades of pink, red, and blue which added to the look of eloquence. It was well kept and the lawn was meticulously manicured. It was quite picturesque and obvious that it belonged to Dennis.

Dennis quickly walked around the car and opened the door for her. "Well this is one of the things I wanted to show you. This is one of twelve bed and breakfast suites that I own.

Come on, I would like to give you a mini tour and introduce you to the staff. Leslie was flabbergasted, nodding her head. Dennis had exquisite taste and she was very eager to see the inside.

Before entering, Dennis walked Leslie around the porch and down the path leading into the backyard. It was an ideal place to meditate, read and pray. It was filled with flowers and a few cast iron chairs and a table.

"A perfect place to hang out on a hot day and sip ice tea or Moscato," she giggled, as she wrapped her hand into his arm."

"That sounds like a perfect idea. Come on let's go inside," leading her back toward the house.

"Hi Mr. Hayes," Jacquie said, eyeing Leslie.

"Leslie, this is Jacquie, she is the manager at this house." Jacquie shook Leslie's hand and offered her a tour of the house.

"No, actually, I will take her on a quick tour and in the mean time, could you fix us a glass of our special ice tea. We would like it in the backyard, please."

"Of course Mr. Hayes, Jacquie said smiling. She is a very pretty young lady. I wonder if this is his girlfriend. "Well, whoever she is, she must be special because he has never brought anyone here before; and now having me to bring them ice tea in the backyard," she scoffed.

Leslie was beyond words, the Bed and Breakfast Suite were beautifully decorated. It reflected Dennis' superb taste all throughout. It makes sense now she thought. She had just sold him Paradise Pillows top-of-the-line linen for each of his suites. Dennis introduced Leslie to Veronica and Peppur as well. It was hard to believe the three ladies took care of the whole house and the guests. They cooked and cleaned and catered to the needs of each guest. Each shared the responsibilities and they worked very well together in giving superb hospitality. Dennis loved each of them. He felt lucky to have such a responsible staff who needed no supervision. They loved him too.

Jacquie could no longer remain silent. "Mr. Hayes, who is this pretty lady? Will she be staying with us?" Veronica and Peppur were just as curious and were happy Jacquie asked. They all focused in to listen to his answer.

"Oh, Leslie works for Paradise Pillows. She is Teresa's assistant. Teresa is on vacation and Nate sent Leslie to sell me their top of the line linen we need. I brought her here to see one of the homes. You all remember Teresa and Nate Bishop, right?"

"Oh sure, of course," Jacquie said, while Veronica and Peppur nodded feeling a little uncomfortable.

"Well, thank you ladies very much for the iced tea. Leslie and I have to get back."

Standing up, Leslie said, "Yes, Dennis, I am ready. It was nice to meet all of you ladies. I enjoyed the ice tea as well. I can tell you all take great pride in your jobs; the house looks amazing, like a picture in a magazine. If I ever come to the Jersey Shore and need a place to stay, I will definitely come here. Thank you ladies, you really made me feel special."

"You are welcome. This is what we do," said Jacquie, giving her a quick wink. "Mr. Hayes would have it no other way." They all laughed.

Dennis escorted Leslie back to the car. "Okay" he said, "one more stop."

Leslie was looking forward to seeing another of Dennis's Bed and Breakfast Suites. "I love this house. The ladies were very nice too. Okay, where are we off to now?' she inquired.

"Yes, they are a great trio. In fact all of the staff is wonderful. I am so lucky to have a group who work really hard in making my business the best. They promote job security," he chuckled.

Dennis deliberately did not answer her as to where they were off to next. He wanted it to be a surprise. Leslie assumed they were at another one of his Bed and Breakfast Suites, when they pulled up in front of a large brick home with double pillars on the porch. There was nothing similar to the Bed and Breakfast Suite, but it looked affluent and stately.

A tall, middle-aged, very attractive woman came out. She looked very happy, as if she was expecting us. Did Dennis call her and tell her we were coming? Is she the manager of this Bed and Breakfast? Leslie wondered.

Dennis smiled and waved as he opened the door for Leslie. The energy flowing from Dennis and the tall attractive woman was contagious. It was warm and comforting. Leslie felt very much at ease as she walked towards the woman smiling.

"Hi Dennis. Wow, who is this beautiful lady?" she inquired.

"This is Leslie Stamford. She is a Sales Consultant for Paradise Pillows. I just purchased some linen for the Bed and Breakfast Suites. She lives in New York and I thought I would show her around and while she is here I wanted her to meet you."

Leslie was really puzzled now. "Who is this woman? Why are we here?" she thought.

"Hello Leslie, I am Gloria Hayes, reaching out to shake her hand. I am Dennis's mother. Please, come on inside."

Shocked and perplexed, Leslie could not believe that Dennis would bring her to meet his mother. "This happens when someone is serious and talking marriage. Surely we have not advanced to that level in 48 hours," she thought.

Glancing through the home, Leslie thought, this home is furnished very nicely as well. Gloria was a gracious hostess. "Please join me in the kitchen. I was just preparing dinner and walked outside to get some fresh air when you guys drove up. May I get you something to drink?" she asked.

"No thanks, Mom. Nothing for me," he answered, looking at Leslie.

"No thank you m'am. We just had some awesome iced tea at the Bed and Breakfast," Leslie said.

She and Gloria had a great time talking and getting to know each other. They stayed and talked for about an hour. It was very obvious that Dennis had deliberately brought her there for a purpose. He hardly did any talking. In fact, he excused himself for a few minutes. He went into his apartment and got the beautiful box he had purchased on his 30th birthday. He concealed the box and took it to his car. It was easy to see him because the convertible top was still down as they both watched him from the window. He appeared to put something in the glove compartment and locked it. They continued to converse. Gloria was very charming and interesting. She shared a few of her own life lessons with Leslie in hopes to get her to relax and open up a bit about herself. She casually asked many questions. Leslie talked about herself and her ambitions in life, her family, and her job. She felt very comfortable conversing with Gloria. They even shared a few laughs. Gloria concluded that Leslie seemed to have great wisdom beyond her years. She could hardly wait to speak with Dennis when he returns home. He has never brought anyone to the house to meet me before. Was this the special woman he had always waited for?

Dennis came back in smiling. Gloria knew he was up to something, but what? "Well, Leslie I hate to break up this party. You and my mother seem to really enjoy each other, but I got to get you back to the Edison tonight. Mom, I practically kidnapped her and brought her here. I wanted to show her a few of the Bed and Breakfast Suites over on Lexington Boulevard and thought I would surprise you too. We have to finish up our business tonight when we get back. I will probably get a room for myself at the Edison and see her off tomorrow."

"Well if there is no rush, why don't you guys stay for dinner?" Gloria beamed.

"Mother, that is sweet and thanks for offering but we need to get back. We will get something to eat on the way."

"Okay Son, See you tomorrow," as she leaned in to give him a hug. "Leslie, it was a real pleasure to meet you. I hope to see you again," as she gave her a warm hug too.

"Yes, m'am, I feel the same way. Thank you so much for having me and thank you Dennis for bringing me here. It has been a wonderful day and I really enjoyed chatting with you, Ms. Hayes."

Dennis waved and winked at his mother as he and Leslie drove away. Gloria knew he was up to something, but what?

CHAPTER 22

Teresa woke up early Monday morning, still feeling a little sad as she remembered crying herself to sleep after reading a few of Ricky's letters. Trying to move on with her life and day, she called Nate Bishop and left a message that she will not be in today, but will be in tomorrow. If he needed her, she was home and can be reached there. She prepared a nice breakfast for Jamie and decided to take him to school. She hoped the nice vacation with Troy was just what Jamie needed to get back on track at school.

As she was driving back to her apartment she decided she was going to stay in all day and finish reading all of Ricky's letters, before calling Momma King. She could hardly wait to tell her all about her vacation with Troy. Oh, yes, she remembered Momma King telling her that she had something to tell her when she came back.

"I hope she remembered to record her teachings on the gifts of the Holy Spirit. She is such a powerful woman of God. I can hardly wait to hear it," she thought. "Oh well, first things first. I am going to get rid of Ricky's ghost that keeps me bound and feeling depressed. I will read all the letters and be done with Ricky Clay once and for all. In my heart I know I still love him, but I can't go on like this. It is not fair to me or Jamie. I must let go," she cried out loud, trying to convince herself.

Just as Teresa came into her apartment, the phone rang. "Hello?" she inquired.

"Hi Teresa, it's Nate. I just got your message that you will not be in today. Are you okay?"

"Oh, yes, Nate. I am feeling great. I just thought I would take another day to unwind, put away things and have a 'me' day. I don't want to seem ungrateful after all you have done for me, but…"

"No, no, no Teresa," Nate said, interrupting her. "Please, if you need a few more days, it is okay. Take as much time as you need. I can't wait to hear all about your vacation. We miss you of course, but we are doing okay. I sent Leslie to sell some of our high end linen to Dennis Hayes in New Jersey last week and she is here today."

"Oh, yes, Mr. Hayes, the owner of several Bed and Breakfast Suites? Yes, I remember. Did she make a good deal for you?"

"Yes, I am quite pleased. She did very well. So, how are you and Jamie really doing?"

"Nate, we really are doing good and thank you again for you and your wife's generosity. We both seem to be in a better place now. I will be in tomorrow. How is Mrs. Bishop?"

Nate was relieved to hear her, and also that she sounded like the "old" Teresa.

"She is doing well. I will tell her you asked about her. Okay, well I look forward to seeing you tomorrow, but if you need some more time just say so."

"No, no, I will see you all tomorrow Nate," she insisted. "Thanks again for calling to check on me."

"No problem, you take care."

"Okay thanks Nate. Bye."

As Teresa was hanging up the phone, she noticed the phone flashing. I gotta listen to my messages before I forget again, then I will settle in to read the letters and call Momma King later.

She pressed the button to hear the messages. There were two messages. First message:

"Hi Sweetie, it's me, Momma King. I just came back from church tonight and I know you just left on your vacation, but please call me as soon as you get this message. It's urgent!!"

Oh, I wonder what this is all about. She told me she had something to tell me when I return from my vacation. I wonder what is so important that she did not tell me before I left with Troy. Alright I will give her a call now.

Next message: "Hi Teresa, It's Leslie Stamford. I just wanted you to know that Dennis Hayes, and I hit it off really well and he is taking me out. Can you believe that? I will fill you in on this Monday when you come back to work."

"Oh my goodness! Oh my goodness... Leslie and Dennis? Unbelievable!! Teresa was completely stunned and took a seat near the phone. Oh wow, I am really happy for her. Dennis Hayes and Leslie Stamford going out on a date! Teresa had known Dennis for over five years and suddenly realized she did not know anything about him. He was always very business-like and focused. He was a great negotiator and seemed to know exactly what he wanted. And Leslie, well she always wanted someone special but no one seemed to meet her qualifications. It has been a long time since she went on a date. I can hardly wait to talk to...

Ring, Ring.

"Hello?"

"Hi Sweetie. I hope I didn't wake you."

"No Momma King I was just going to call you. What's wrong?"

"Can you come over here right away? If you are too tired I will be over in a few minutes."

"Huh? Uh, Okay. Momma King you can come over. Are you okay?"

"Yes, put on some hot water for some tea. See you in a few minutes," she said, hastily hanging up the phone.

Perplexed and confused, Teresa slowly walked to the kitchen and put the hot water on. "What could it be that would warrant Momma King to rush over here? What has happened since Jamie and I went on vacation seven days ago. What could not wait until later this evening? Jamie and Troy and I were planning on getting in on the last two nights of Momma King's teaching. What has happened that she must see me right away?" she wondered.

Teresa set the table for tea and heated the oven to bake a few croissants. Momma King arrived and brushed past Teresa. She settled down at the table. Teresa watched her very carefully as she poured her a cup of tea and served the croissants.

"Momma King, what has gotten you in such a tizzy?" Teresa asked.

"Teresa, last Sunday night when I finished teaching, I got the shock of my life. I am not sure how to tell you, but Jamie's father is here and ..."

"What? Jamie's father? Michael Hayden? Are you sure Momma King?" Teresa screamed. "What is he doing here? What did he say? Where is he?"

"Whoa, Whoa," Teresa calm down. "Please, I will tell you everything." Momma King could not tell if she was happy, angry, or in utter distress, but she knew she had to hurry and reveal what she knew.

"He has been here for a week now. He is staying at the church and Pastor Sherman is preparing him for ministry."

"What? Ministry? Michael?"

"Yes, Sweetie. He came to the church while I was teaching on miracles. Afterwards he came to me and told me that it was a miracle he was there. He said God literally directed him to the Light of Love Church by a vision he had earlier. I knew he looked familiar but I could not place him at first. He looks very different now. He said he came here looking for you last Sunday right after you left and said one of your neighbors told him you and Jamie were on vacation. He wanted to come over to my house to find out about you and Jamie the past nine years. I told him he needs to speak with you first and then if you

ALL wanted to come to my house, I would be okay with that. I was not going to tell him anything." Momma King declared.

"I can't believe he is here. I have heard absolutely nothing from him since Jamie was born and now he shows up nine years later and wants to know how we made out. I have nothing to say to him now," she said, with great resentment."

"Teresa, I know you are not happy about this, but you are now a born-again Christian and you have to forgive him. I think he is truly sorry which is why he is here. Just hear him out honey. It may be good for the both of you to bring closure in some way now that you both are new creatures in Christ," Momma King counseled.

Just then the doorbell rang. They both sat frozen to their seats. Suddenly the phone rang out, causing both of them to jump.

"Okay Teresa," Momma King said. "You get the door and I will get the phone, pushing herself away from the table to answer the phone."

"Hello?"

The door bell rang again. Teresa's heart was pounding loudly in her ears. She was having a hard time breathing. She knew it was Michael on the other side of the door, and she was not ready to deal with him. What was she going to say? No, I don't have to answer the door. He can't just show up here without calling or getting my permission. Teresa was suddenly so angry she jumped up from the table and marched over to the door and ...

"Oh, hi Troy, it's me, Mrs. King. Ahhh, Teresa is...Ahhh, yes, Teresa is tied up right now, but I will have her call you back as soon as she is free."

"Is everything alright, Mrs. King?"

"Yes Troy. Everything is fine. She will call you back. Someone is at the door."

"Oh Okay, Mrs. King. I will probably see you tonight at church. You have two more nights to teach on the gifts of the Holy Spirit, right?"

"Yes, Troy, I am looking forward to seeing you there."

"Okay, tell Teresa I will pick her and Jamie up for church tonight."

"Yes, yes, of course I will let her know."

"Okay. Bye now."

Momma King hung up the phone and began to pray. *"Lord, please help Teresa have the right attitude while she is dealing with her past. Renew the right spirit in her, in Jesus name."*

And....there he was! Michael stood smiling with a huge bouquet of multi-colored flowers. They were beautiful. Teresa was confused and had mixed emotions. Should I slap him or kiss him or kick him? Should I hurt him like he hurt me? Teresa stepped back from the open door, leaving just enough space for him to walk in. He took that as an invitation to enter and he did.

He had matured handsomely and smelled very masculine. He had a full black beard. It was Michael; but, a different Michael indeed, she thought.

Momma King broke the silence, "well we meet again Michael and it is nice to see you. I guess I will be leaving now. Teresa, I will talk to you later. Oh, and give Troy a call. Teresa?"

Momma King noticed that Teresa had not said a word since she opened the door.

"Teresa? Are you okay? Did you hear me?" she said, staring into her visibly perplexed face.

"Ahh, Yes M'am. Okay. I will call you later," she said, still standing with the door open, as if in a daze.

"No, I said give Troy a call. That was him on the phone."

Momma King hugged her as she walked out the door. She realized Teresa did not hear a word she said. She physically took the door knob out of Teresa's hand, and nodded to Michael while closing the door as she left.

"Wow, Teresa you look amazing," Michael said smiling and offering her the flowers.

"Humph! Please," She sneered and dismissed his compliment.

She took the flowers, passing him as she walked into the kitchen to get a large vase.

"Okay. Teresa, I know I am the last person you expected to see, but I came back here to New York to tell you I am sorry for what I did and to make some things right with you and Jamie. Could you please sit down and allow me to talk a bit?"

"Are you kidding me Michael? Making things right after nine years…how do you plan to do that?" she sneered.

"Please, Teresa, can you please sit down with me and talk?" he pleaded.

"You show up here at my apartment unannounced and now want me to take the time out of my schedule to entertain someone who is not considerate of me or my time. You made your choice nine years ago when you walked out on me and your newborn son. Now you show up nine years later and want to talk? How silly does that sound Michael?" she screamed. "In fact, I think you should leave now."

"No, please, Teresa, please hear me out. His voice became desperate. Please, Teresa, I am very sorry I hurt you and left you. I was such a coward and afraid of responsibility. God sent me back here...please Teresa, I am not the same man that left you to raise my son all alone. Please, please, sit down and let me talk to you." He began to cry uncontrollably.

Teresa became malleable and offered him a chair. He did seem to be genuinely remorseful.

"Okay Michael, have a seat. Please stop crying. Do you want some hot tea and croissants?"

"Yes, that will be fine if it is not too much trouble," he said, sniffling and reaching into his pocket for his handkerchief to dry his eyes.

"This is truly a sight to behold, Michael crying and sobbing. "My! My! My! This is how he left me...nine years ago, crying and sobbing." This is a different man than what I remembered. "Okay, I will hear him out," she thought.

She poured him and herself a cup of tea and took a seat opposite him. "Help yourself to the croissants. You want butter or jelly or anything else?"

"No, thank you Teresa. This is fine." He paused and looked away from her piercing eyes for a moment.

"Okay Teresa, I am here this morning because I wanted to ask you to please forgive me. I have so much on my heart that I will ask if you could please not yell and scream at me until I am able to tell you everything I came here to tell you. Okay?"

Teresa nodded.

"Well, I realized that I was a coward and a poor excuse of a man. After I walked out on you, I moved to Austin, Texas with the woman I started to hang out with before I left. I never loved her, but she was convenient and wanted to move away. So, I ran from my responsibilities because I was afraid I would fail at being a good father and too immature and selfish to do the right thing and marry you and be a good husband. So I ran. I think it was guilt and fear that made me work so hard. I started my own trucking business because I was afraid to work for someone for fear of someone firing me. I was able to establish a very successful business, but I have been absolutely miserable.

Sometime, I would have to take long drives to take care of business deals. I had a lot of time on my hand to think about my life and what had become of it. Sometimes, I would listen to the radio and one day, a few months ago, I heard a preacher say, "A man who does not take care of his own is worse than an infidel." That haunted me every day. I thought of you and Jamie so much; I couldn't take it anymore. I gave up everything in Austin to come back here to do the right thing by you and Jamie. On my way here, my engine blew. I met a State Trooper

163

who led me to the Lord and shared his amazing testimony of how God delivered him from alcoholism and restored his marriage. His story was remarkable and it encouraged me while I waited for the tow truck. The tow truck took me about 20 miles off the main highway to a mechanic. I ended up with a hillbilly named Charlie in the backwoods of Texas. It was as if God had orchestrated my footsteps. I was forced to stay with him for one week while he replaced my engine. There were no hotels, motels or anything remotely like such. It was very isolated and lacking. I have never seen someone who had nothing, but was happy and content with just having Jesus. He shared everything he had with me. God brought me to my knees and taught me so many things about myself while I was there. I learned that money and success did not give me the peace and contentment that Charlie had. He had nothing. He lived off the land and worked on cars. His one room shack was divided by sheets hanging up by ropes separating his living room from his big potbelly stove. He had two old plates and a knife, two spoons and a large fork. He offered me part of his dinner that night."

Michael paused as his voice began to tremble and his eyes swelled with tears again as he reflected.

"It was muskrat and swamp cabbage and a sweet potato. I was horrified, but before the week was out, I was humble and grateful for whatever foods he shared with me. He was happy and thankful. Afterwards, he worshipped God and prayed for me

164

and mentored me in the Word of God. Just before I left, his pastor came and laid hands on me and I had a vision. I saw myself preaching all over the world and then I saw a sign that read 'Light of Love Ministries' in a flaming fire. The words were very clear. When I first arrived here, I came here to see you. After I learned that you and Jamie were on vacation, I got in my truck to find a hotel room. I am still in awe because the next thing I knew I was in front of a church, Light and Love Ministries. The words were lit up in a flaming fire again. Just like the vision I had earlier. I went in and that is when I saw Ms. King. She was teaching on miracles. This whole experience since I left Texas has been a miracle. I know God is doing something great with my life. When I met Pastor Sherman, he told me that God had instructed him to mentor me. He is preparing me to preach the message of salvation to the nations. I have been staying there at the church and being mentored daily. Pastor Sherman is such an inspiration and great man of God. I don't know all that God has planned for me, but I want you and Jamie to be a part of it. I know this is a lot to take in and a lot to ask, but I am a changed man and I want to take care of you and Jamie; if you will allow me. Teresa, I left New York as a boy, I have returned a man. I don't know what you have been through or had to deal with all alone these past nine years, but I'm here now. I want to make things right with God, you and Jamie. I am going to be here for a while and would like to meet my son and get to know him."

His voice was now just above a whisper and all of Teresa's anger was gone and replaced with great compassion. Michael gently reached across the table and held her hands. "Let's pray together, is that okay?" Teresa could only nod her head as tears filled her eyes.

They both cried and prayed. The presence of God filled the apartment. She could see clearly he was a changed man indeed. His forceful and compelling testimony had given Teresa goose bumps.

CHAPTER 23

Leslie and Dennis enjoyed dinner and a stroll in the park before returning to the hotel. Dennis had hoped she would have stayed at one of his Bed and Breakfasts, in New Jersey, but decided against asking her for fear of her being offended at the suggestion. "Well, it is no big deal," he thought, "I already took care of everything so she can stay another night here at the Edison."

They entered the hotel around 9PM. Dennis did not want the night to end. He heard the jazz band playing in the lounge and suggested a night cap.

"Oh, that sounds wonderful," Leslie said smiling. "I really enjoyed being with you today. I can't remember when I have had so much fun."

"You are deserving, pretty lady. I really enjoyed being with you as well," he said as he opened the door of the lounge.

A few couples were up dancing to the jazzy sounds of Will Downing. The atmosphere was quixotic and complimented the newly love-struck moods of Leslie and Dennis. They took the round table near the dance floor. Dennis signaled the waitress.

"Leslie, what would you like to drink?" He asked.

"I would like Drambuie on the rocks!"

"Now, that's a pretty big drink for such a little lady," he teased.

"Hey, don't worry, I can handle it, she laughed, thinking he may be right, reflecting on the buzz she got from the Moscato she had yesterday.

Dennis stayed with his usual martini. They danced and had several more drinks. By midnight they were considerably intoxicated and the lounge was almost empty. Leslie was beyond woozy and decided it was time for her to go to her room and sleep it off. "Dennis, she said, through slurred pauses of laughter, "you are everything a woman could possibly ask for and I am glad I met you but I think you were right…Drambuie is a pretty big drink for a little lady. I am kinda wiped out!" Giggling as she attempted to stand up, Dennis laughed. "She is the cutest little thing" he thought and quickly helped her up.

"Okay, no problem, let's get you to your room and I will … Oh, wow, I forgot to get a room for myself. Well, it is not a problem. We can stop at the front desk and get a room for me on our way up to your room. Is that okay?"

"Sure, no problem, the walking is probably good for me," she said holding tightly to his arm. Juella, the front desk check-in clerk asked, "May I help you?"

"Yes, I would like a room for the night please," Dennis said, reaching for his credit card.

"Oh, I'm sorry sir, but we are completely booked. We have no vacancies."

Dennis heart sank. "What? No rooms? Are you sure?"

"Yes sir, I am sorry, but it is after midnight and I am sure no one will be checking out until check out time tomorrow," she said, sympathizing at his predicament.

"Oh," Leslie queried, "Do you have a cot that we can add to my room?"

"Yes, we can get a cot into your room. Letting out a sigh of relief, Juella was glad they both will be staying because they looked to inebriated to drive. What is your name please?"

"Leslie Stamford. Room 714." She answered turning to face Dennis, "you can stay in my room as long as you promise to behave and stay on the cot," she said giggling.

"Ms. Stamford, I just called room service and they will be right there with an extra Cot."

"Thank you," she said.

"Okay, let's go 'Mr. Forgetful,' she teased, holding tightly to his arm. "Let's go to our room."

CHAPTER 24

Teresa and Michael spent the rest of the afternoon getting reacquainted. Michael shared with Teresa pretty much everything that happened the past nine years of his life. He told of his relationship with Tavia and how that relationship failed because he did not love her. He always felt guilty for abandoning her and Jamie. Teresa shared her ordeal and admitted she was still in love with Ricky but was trying to move forward. She shared how much Jamie loved Ricky and the time they spent together and how he had been acting out in school since he left. Michael blamed himself for not being there for them. They cried and prayed together.

"Please forgive me Teresa, I have a lot of making up to do to you both," he said as tears streamed down his face. He reached out and touched her hand. Teresa embraced his gesture of compassion. She could not believe how comfortable she had become with Michael. It was almost like old times. He was very open and honest; still very handsome and charismatic. She loved his beard. It made him look more masculine and mature. His style of dressing was western, but very appealing.

Feeling a little awkward, Teresa pulled her hand away. "Oh, my Mike, Jamie is due home in two hours and I have not gotten anything done today," she exclaimed.

"I am sorry," said Michael. "I guess I should leave now, but will it be alright if I meet Jamie today?"

"Well, I think it would be a good idea if you leave now and come back this evening around 6PM to have dinner with us. It will give me a little time to seek God and prepare Jamie to meet you. I can make your favorite dish if I remember correctly; Fried chicken, mashed potatoes and gravy with string beans right?"

"Yes, but you forgot the cornbread, he chuckled. "Is it too much to ask?" he wondered.

"No, not at all, but when you leave I need you to go to the All in All grocery store and get the chicken, potatoes, string beans and the cornbread mix. I still have eggs in the fridge. Jamie and I just got back yesterday from a week's vacation and I have not been able to get to the store yet," she responded.

"Of course, I will be back in a few minutes. I will make sure I get back before Jamie comes. Thank you, Teresa. Thank you for forgiving me. It means the world to me." He stood and kissed her on the forehead.

"Okay, I will see you in a few minutes," as he walked out the door.

Teresa had forgotten she had promised Momma King that she and Jamie and Troy, would be at church to hear her teach the last two nights on the gifts of the Holy Spirit. She had also forgotten to call Troy back as Momma King informed her before leaving.

Teresa sat in a daze for the next forty-five minutes. She kept reflecting on their conversation and how he made her feel inside. She felt his love and genuineness. It took her back to the days before she got pregnant with Jamie. They had shared a great relationship, but when she became pregnant everything changed. She knew he did not want children, but it was not like she could send it back. And to consider an abortion as Michael suggested was not an option for her. Michael, afraid of the responsibility of raising a child abandoned them both. She knew she too was a changed woman. God had taken away her old stony and broken heart that was filled with hurt and unforgiveness and replaced it with a heart that was sensitive to His Spirit. She felt no anger or animosity toward him at all. Could she still be in love with him and have suppressed it for nine years? What is going on with me? This is ridiculous or was it?" She asked herself.

Teresa was still in the same place in deep thought when Michael returned. He had an arm full of groceries and several more bags in the car.

"I hope this will save you a trip to the store. I tried to think of everything so you won't have to go out," he stated.

Teresa smiled and waved him into the kitchen to set the bags on the counter.

"That was very sweet of you Michael, but you did not have to go to all that trouble."

"What? Are you kidding me? No trouble at all. It was a pleasure and a greater pleasure knowing I will be back later to eat some of it with you and my son. Teresa you have no idea how grateful I am that you are being so kind to me. I truly thank God for you being so nice. You have always been such a beautiful woman, inside and out and I can tell you've been an outstanding momma too. Thank you Teresa."

Teresa quickly moved out of his arm reach. She felt vulnerable and definitely did not want him to hug her or attempt to kiss her on her forehead again.

"Thanks Mike, but God gets all the glory here," smiling shyly. She moved quickly into the kitchen putting away the things he had brought, avoiding close contact.

173

Michael sensed her uneasiness and headed towards the door.

"Well I better run now so you can get yourself situated before Jamie comes. I will see you both at 6PM."

"Yes, Mike, that will be great. Thanks again for the groceries and we will see you later," as she busied herself in the kitchen.

She had just an hour before Jamie got home. "I must go into my bedroom to talk to my heavenly father. I need some real godly wisdom because my emotions are all over the place right now. I don't trust myself. Oh, before I pray, I will give Momma King a quick call. She always seems to know what to do," she determined.

Ring, Ring!

"Hello Momma King, it's me Teresa."

"I know sweetie. I've been praying for you. Are you okay?"

"Yes Momma King. I feel happy and yet I feel confused. I had such a nice time talking with Michael. He is a changed man and wants to do right by me and Jamie now. I am not mad at him. I don't feel any anger, and I am confused by that because of all that he did to me; is it normal for me to still feel....love for him?" she inquired.

"Oh my dear child yes, it is perfectly normal to feel love for him because of Christ who lives on the inside of you now. God has renewed the right Spirit in you. I am so proud of you, and what God has done in your heart. So, what are you going to do now?"

"Well, he will be over later to meet Jamie and have dinner with us. I am feeling excited but nervous too because he keeps saying he wants to take care of me and Jamie and I am not so sure what he really means," she answered.

"I am sure the Lord knows. He will reveal to you exactly what he means. Just stay in and attitude of prayer and watch everything closely. Sometimes you can learn so much about a person and their motives just by watching and listening. So, pay attention and listen for God's small voice deep within you."

Yes M'am…thanks Momma King.

"Oh, don't forget to call Troy. He said he will be by to pick you and Jamie up for the teaching tonight!"

Teresa's heart sank.

"Oh my goodness! I forgot. Mike is coming over for dinner and Troy is coming to take us to church! What am I going to do? I can't call Mike to cancel because I don't have his number. I know he is staying in the guest quarters at the church and that number is different from the church's main number."

"Well you could call Troy, right?" Momma King suggested.

"Yes, and tell him my ex-boyfriend showed up who has been missing for nine years and I can't go to church with you because Jamie and I are having dinner with him tonight?" she said sarcastically.

"I do understand Sweetie, but that is the truth as crude as it may be." Momma King added.

"I can't hurt Troy like that. He has been so wonderful to us, and Jamie has become very fond of him. I am going to call him. Hopefully I can think of something that is not a blatant lie. Momma King, I gotta run now. Oh, you said you had something you wanted to tell me this morning. What was it?"

"Oh, it can wait sweetie. You got a lot going on right now. I can tell you later."

"Yes, we can talk later and if I don't make it to church tonight, could you please record the teaching for me again?" Teresa asked.

"Sure, I will have Les record it for you again. Oops, I slipped," she mumbled under her breath.

"What? Les? Who is Les?"

"Teresa I can tell you all of this later, it is not important right now. You need to figure out what you are doing. So, handle your business and we can talk later. I gotta run too. Love you. Bye."

Momma King hung up abruptly to avoid any more questions about her new love, Judge Les Harris. She wanted the moment to be right when she told her and hopefully she would like him as well. Even though he was pretty tough on her in his courtroom, but fair, she affirmed in his defense. I pray she will be happy for me and let by-gones be by-gones. Her opinion of my new friend does matter a lot because I love her and Jamie so much. It will not be a deal breaker if they don't, but it will make the relationship much easier for everyone, she thought.

Teresa quickly hung up the phone and immediately called Troy.

Ring, Ring!

"Hello you have reached the Law office of Troy Kennedy. Today is Monday, It is twelve noon and I will be out of the office the remainder of the day. Please call back tomorrow between 9 and 5 and be sure to leave your name and number at the sound of the beep and I will call you back as soon as possible. Thank you for calling."

Teresa hung up. She realized she only had his office number and not his home number. Just as she was trying to figure out what to do next Jamie came busting through the door. Oh, no, I did not get a chance to pray yet. *"Lord, please help me and give me wisdom in everything. May I handle myself and the sensitivity of this matter pleasingly to you, in Jesus name. Amen.*

"Hey Mom! It smells good in here. I smell fried chicken. Yummy! Can I have a piece now?"

"No not right now, but how about some milk and cookies?"

"Oh alright," he answered.

"So how was your day in school?"

"It was good Momma. I had a good day. It was "show and tell" day. We had to tell what we did on our spring break. I showed the postcards I got from the country club. Everyone loved the pictures and asked me did I actually go fishing, rock climbing, skating and swimming. A lot of the kids did not do anything. Some stayed home and cleaned out their garages. Everybody was asking me questions about my vacation with you and Troy. Momma, can we go back again and can I bring two of my friends from school?" He shrieked with excitement.

"Well, we will see Jamie. I am glad you had a good day today. Your classmates made you feel really special, I can see

178

that. I am very happy for you Jamie. But come here and sit with me for a minute. I need to talk to you about something."

"What's wrong Momma?"

"Well, nothing is wrong, but I think it will be great news for you."

Jamie's eyes widened with excitement. "What Momma, Ricky is back?! Tell me!" He insisted.

"No Sweetie, It is not about Ricky. Sit down here at the table. I will be right back."

Jamie was deeply disappointed, but still curious.

"Mama tell me," he whined.

Teresa came back with a glass of milk and freshly baked chocolate chip cookies that Michael had just purchased for them.

Jamie studied his Momma's face. "Okay Mom, what is it?" He asked.

Well, remember, you always asked me who was your real daddy?"

"Yes, M'am."

"Your daddy came back and wants to meet you. He came here today and we had a long talk. He is coming over tonight for dinner."

"Are you happy Momma?"

"Well the question should be are you happy your daddy came back?"

"I really don't care. Ricky has been my daddy and he will be back soon. I don't need another daddy."

Teresa was surprised by his reaction. She really did not think that he would have a negative reaction. He had a great day in school and he seems to be back on track feeling good about himself again. *"O God please don't let this upset Jamie. Help us both to deal with this in Jesus name."*

"Maybe you can at least meet him. I think you will really like him. You look a lot like him," she said trying to coax him into a least being receptive.

"Okay Momma. Do you like him?"

"Yes, of course. Give him a chance okay?"

"Yes, M'am."

"I am going to take a quick shower and change my clothes. I smell like fresh garlic and fried chicken."

Jamie frowned and laughed.

CHAPTER 25

Leslie and Dennis made it to their shared hotel room, wobbling all the way. Room service had already put the cot in the room for Dennis. Both having had too much to drink, things quickly escalated and there was no longer a need for a cot. They shared the bed as well as each other. Leslie woke up first, naked and ashamed. She ran into the bathroom and began to shower. She began to cry. Suddenly, Dennis was standing right behind her, naked as well. He hugged her and begged her to please stop crying. He was not so proud of himself either.

"We both had way too much to drink and it is all my fault."

"No, it was not all your fault, Leslie said as she turned to face him. I should not have had so much to drink. Drambuie is a very powerful scotch liqueur. It was way too strong for me and I am so embarrassed. Now, I am standing in the shower naked with a man I have only known for 48 hours. I am so ashamed."

"Okay, this may not be natural, but it feels natural. You are a beautiful woman Leslie and nothing about my feelings has changed."

He pulled her close to him. The hot water quickly steamed up the room creating a foggy mist. Leslie was caught up in the moment but adamant that having sexual relations with Dennis couldn't happen again. Not like this, she thought.

"Dennis I am sorry, but this is inappropriate and I have to go," pushing the shower curtain back and wrapping herself in the towel that hung nearest to her. Once in the room, she removed the towel and quickly looked around for her clothes. She found them under the covers at the foot of the bed. She dressed as fast as she could. She had to get away. She was beyond embarrassment and humiliation.

Dennis came out of the bathroom wrapped in a towel. His muscular frame was too much to take in. Leslie lowered her eyes. Wow, he is some kind of sexy," she thought, I definitely must go. I know I have not been with a man in several years, but I did not expect to act like a "loose woman" the first time alone with such a hunk of a man.

"Leslie, remember the other day when I first met you asked you did you believe in love at first sight?"

"Yes, I remember, Leslie said, looking perplexed.

"And remember I said I know this may seem like I am moving too fast and I don't want to run you away, but I want you to know I meant what I said. I have waited for a long time for that special lady, and with everything in me...I feel and know, I have found her."

Leslie remained frozen and did not answer. "And you asked if you had any say in the matter and I told you not to answer then, but tomorrow. Well today is tomorrow. Will you please answer me now."

Dennis walked over to his jacket and removed something from his pocket and moved over to face Leslie. He kneeled in front of her and produced a huge solitaire four carat diamond ring. Looking deep into her eyes, he asked, "Will you be my woman for life?"

Leslie was speechless! Tears streamed down her face but nothing came out of her mouth. She began to hyperventilate.

Dennis stood up and helped her to sit on the bed. Her breathing was very rapid and tears continued to flow down her cheeks. Dennis found a bottle of sparkling water in the refrigerator. He quickly opened it and insisted she take a sip of it.

Leslie took a big gulp. She choked initially, but the coughing subsided and her breathing became steady. Dennis sat next to her and rubbed her back. Leslie laid her head on his shoulder, as tears continued to swell in her eyes. They stayed in that same position a long time. Finally, Dennis lifted her face to his and kissed her ever so gently. "You never answered me. I know it is very short. I am more than confident that you are the one for me. Are you willing to take this chance with me? I promise to always take care of you. I want you to be the mother of my children. I want you Leslie…will you be my woman for life?"

Leslie, still crying, looked into his eyes. Yes, only if the ring fits. If it fits then I know it is for me.

Dennis was surprised at her response. He always said the same thing in his mind. He smiled, feeling confident it would fit, he teased, "okay, Cinderella, I know you are not one of her ugly sisters, so let's try it on.

Leslie laughed nervously through her fountain of tears and put out her finger.

"See Cinderella, it fits perfectly. Looks like God already knew this would be for you. I bought it three years ago for the special woman that I planned to marry. It all worked out well and I was able to get the ring when I brought you home to meet my mother. Leslie, I know I love you. I just know deep inside you are my wife."

Leslie gasped at the huge rock sitting perfectly on her finger. "Is this a dream? Have I finally found the love of my life? He is everything any woman could want and it feels so right. Some people may think it is too soon," she thought, "but she quickly dismissed the thought of what others may think. What others think is their business. This is our business and I am willing to take the chance and go with my heart.

"It's beautiful Dennis. I love it and I don't know exactly how to express what I feel, but I felt it the first day I saw you standing at the fountain. I never really gave it much thought to even consider if love at first sight is real, but I guess it's true. I know I never want what I feel now to ever end," she said, and "Yes, Dennis I would love to be your woman for life!"

Dennis gave a big sigh of relief and kissed her over and over, but, stopped abruptly. He did not want her to feel she should have sexual relations with him because he had proposed to her. The next time he wanted it to be special and on her terms, and without alcohol playing a part. "Let's have brunch together before we depart from each other. I want to talk about where we go from here," he suggested. "I just want us to be on the same page, since you live in New York and I live in New Jersey."

Leslie said, I have a better idea. Let's spend the rest of the afternoon in bed before we leave. Last night things happened because we both were intoxicated. Today, I want to have some special memories with the man I am going to spend the rest of my life with...Memories I can take with me back to New York, she purred, as she pulled him back on the bed.

"Yes, yes, I think that is a wonderful idea," he said as he kissed his wife to be. "Perfect!!"

CHAPTER 26

Teresa noticed Ricky's letters still lying on her bed as she showered and changed her clothes for dinner. It was painful as she remembered crying herself to sleep last night. It was as if the letters were there to torment her, yet she could not resist them. She decided to leave them on the bed and read more before going to bed. But, for now, they will have to wait.

Teresa had just added the fresh flowers as the centerpiece on the table when Michael arrived. He was on time with an overwhelming wealth of gifts for Jamie which he decided to leave in the truck for the moment. There were nine gifts for each year he was absent in Jamie's life. He was visibly nervous as he rang the doorbell. Teresa rushed to open the door to spare Jamie from the awkwardness of facing his father for the first time.

"Hello Mike. Come in."

Michael noticed she had changed her clothes and she looked amazingly beautiful and radiant. Did she make this special appearance for me? Feeling confident that he had won her respect again, he looked past her hoping to lay his eyes on his son. Jamie sat at the table with his back to Michael, appearing to be uninterested.

"Hi Teresa, you look beautiful, he said, as he leaned in and kissed her on the cheek. It smells wonderful in here. I smell all of my favorite foods, just like old times."

"Yes," she thought feeling a little annoyed at his comment of 'like old times.'

"Go on in and have a seat. Jamie! Jamie! Come here please," she called.

Jamie turned around from his chair eyeing Michael with caution as he walked over to his mother. "Jamie, this is your dad. His name is Michael."

"Hi," Jamie said, as he extended his hand avoiding eye contact.

"Hi Jamie, wow you are becoming such a man," he said as he shook his hand. "I am very happy to finally meet you. I brought you some things, but they are so many I am going to need your help to bring them in. Can you give me a hand?"

Jamie's eyes widened with excitement, "Can I ma?"

"No Jamie, maybe after dinner."

Michael appeared to be surprised and it was obvious he felt awkward. He stood still unsure what to do or say.

"Has his guilt and success gotten the best of him so that he is now trying to bribe his son? It is evident that God still has

187

some things to work out within him," she thought trying to keep her composure. She motioned him to take a seat at the table.

"Ma, why not?" Jamie sulked.

"Jamie it is okay. Do what your mother says. Teresa I am sorry, I should have asked if it was okay first."

"Yes, Michael you are right. You should have!" She snapped.

"Well, I guess we are getting off to a good start, huh?" He said, laughing trying to make light of the situation and directing his attention to Jamie. "Jamie, tell me. What do you like to do for fun?"

"I like to go fishing, and Troy just took us on vacation and we went rock climbing. We had a lot of fun on the bumper cars and the speed racing cars, but we could not go too fast because Momma was scared. Jamie laughed. Ricky said I am becoming a man now, so I have to look out for Momma and take care of her."

"Yes, you are Jamie, your mother told me about Ricky, but who is Troy?"

Teresa interjected; he is my friend and my attorney. Now, how about some mashed potatoes?" passing him the bowl and ending the interrogation.

"Yes," taking the hint and settled down to small chit chat with Jamie. He did not seem to have any noticeable effect on Jamie until he confessed that he walked out and left him.

"So why are you here now? You want to be my daddy? Well, I am almost a man now and I don't need a daddy now!" Jamie said sarcastically.

Teresa tried to intervene. "No, Teresa its okay, he is right. Let him have his say. I deserve it and I understand. Jamie you are right and I am sorry. Please forgive me. I was afraid that I would not be a good father to you. I was a coward and I ran from my responsibilities. After growing up and becoming a man, God would not let me rest so I am back because I want to make things right. I made a mistake. I want to be a part of your life."

"Okay" Jamie said. "I forgive you." Momma King and Momma said, "when someone asks you to forgive them you must forgive them; if not Jesus will not forgive you for your sins."

Teresa beamed proudly at Jamie and hearing Mike's dialogue and confession pulled at Teresa's heart again. "Well you two, how about some dessert?" She said, wiping back tears.

"Momma can we have dessert later? I want to go with Michael to help him bring in my presents. Can I Momma please?" Teresa gave Michael a quick look. He nodded with his eyes an unspoken please and thank you.

"Okay you two. Hurry up. I will be in the kitchen cleaning up and getting the dessert."

They came back in with a Huffy bicycle, a skate board, a softball and glove with a bat, a monogrammed Bible with Jamie's name on it, a watch, board games, a miniature pool table and with all the makings for a fifty gallon fish tank.

"Mike what are you doing? Is this nine years of gifts you are trying to make up for? This is over the top Mike and a little ridiculous. Where are all these things supposed to go?" She asked angrily.

"Momma I can put the bike in the hallway and the pool table here in the living room and…"

"Jamie stop! Please!" she said, interrupting him and glaring at Mike.

"Well Teresa listen, how about letting me get you a larger apartment or even a house and yard for Jamie to rip and run in. I can …"

"Stop it Mike, You will do no such thing!" She yelled.

Just then the door bell rang. It was almost 6:45PM. Who can that be she wondered as she walked over to the door?" Still in a funk at Michael, she snatched open the door.

"Troy?" She said stunned. "What are you doing here?"

"Oh, I guess we are not going to church huh?"

"Oh, Troy, I am sorry. I completely forgot. Please come in."

"Wow, what's going on in here? Christmas is here early for someone. I guess I would forget about going to church too with all of these things to play with," he said, smiling at Jamie.

"Hi Troy," Jamie said running to give him a hug.

Michael stood staring at Troy. "Uhmm, Troy this is Michael, Jamie's dad." Teresa mumbled.

Troy stepped in closer and shook his hand. "It's nice to meet you. You have a wonderful son who is super smart and growing up really fast."

"Now, how would you know so much about my son?" Michael snarled.

"Really Mike?" Teresa protested.

"Well, I guess this is not a good time," Troy said to Teresa, dismissing Michael and his comment. "I will talk to you later if that is okay?"

"Yes, of course." She said humiliated.

"Hey Troy, don't leave I want to show you all of my new stuff," Jamie yelled from across the room.

"I would love to Jamie, but we will have to do it another day real soon okay?"

"Okay, Bye Troy."

"Bye Jamie. Enjoy your new toys."

Teresa learned a lot about Troy on their vacation together and she knew he was hurt and disappointed. I can't believe that I totally forgot our commitment to go to church tonight to hear Momma King teach. I hope he doesn't think I preferred Michael over him. Why did Michael become so territorial and disrespectful to Troy? Oh, I feel terrible about this whole thing, but I know one thing...he has overstepped his boundaries and he has to go now!

Teresa made no effort to conceal her anger. "Okay, Mr. Santa Claus, Christmas is over and has been for nine years and I would like very much for you to leave now and please don't make a scene departing. I have to get Jamie ready for school and figure out where to put all this stuff, and, if you decide to buy something else, I would appreciate it if you would speak to me about it first. If you want to spend time with your son, call and confirm when and where with me before coming here again. I hope I have made myself clear."

Surprisingly Jamie did not seem to notice what was said or what was going on. He was enamored with all his new gifts.

"Wait a minute, we didn't have dessert yet," he said trying to get her to smile but to no avail. "Okay Teresa, I am sorry. I didn't mean to upset you...I just..."

"Yeah, yeah, yeah" she said mockingly, waving him off. "Just leave please."

"Okay Teresa, let me say goodnight to my son. Hey Jamie...I gotta go now buddy. Maybe we can get together soon to try out your new fishing pole okay?"

"Okay Bye. Thank you," Jamie said, paying no attention to him, still mesmerized by his influx of toys.

"Good night Teresa" he said, as she stood holding the door open.

"Bye Mike," she said, closing the door as he exited.

CHAPTER 27

Leslie had fallen asleep after spending the afternoon with Dennis. She dreamt she was Cinderella and had met a Prince who fell in love with her and escorted her to the biggest social event of the year. She was the most beautiful woman there, dressed in her finest apparel and was the envy of all the ladies that laid eyes on her. The Prince was enthralled by her beauty and eloquence. They danced all night to the same song "Unforgettable," eyes locked into each other's. Suddenly the Prince kneeled on one knee and placed a big shiny ring on her finger and they continued to dance. She was having so much fun that she forgot she had to be home by midnight. Abruptly the sound of the big grandfather clock struck 12 O'clock. "oh no, no, no, I got to get home she began moaning in her sleep. No, I got to get home."

Dennis shook her lightly. "Leslie, Leslie"...he called her softly. She suddenly opened her eyes and realized she had fallen asleep. Was she dreaming? Had Dennis really proposed to her? Was he the Prince that proposed to me and took me dancing?..."Whew! Yes," she said, "I was dreaming. Trying to make sense of her state of mind, she realized she was naked in bed with a four carat diamond ring on her finger and Dennis smiling lovingly at her. She could not believe all that had happened in the past forty-eight hours.

"Dennis, I hate to leave, but I have to get home. What time is it?" She asked nervously.

"It's almost 5PM. I know baby, but before you leave, I want you to know I am very serious about everything I have said to you. I will come to see you every weekend and if I can break away maybe the middle of the week. I want you to be my wife, and very soon. Here's what I want you to think about. Would you consider relocating to the Jersey Shores and being the mother of my children and my partner in business? I know this is a lot but I know in my heart this is exactly what I want and have waited for. Take your time to think about everything and look deep within your heart to see if this is the same thing you would like. I want to take care of you for the rest of your life. If you say yes, it will be your choice if you want to work or not, I just want you to be happy."

"Dennis, you take my breath away. This all feels like a fairy tale. I just dreamt that I was Cinderella and you were this handsome Prince that literally swept me off my feet and we both were instantly in love as we danced the night away... until I suddenly realized it was midnight and I had to go."

He laughed and said, "Baby that was a beautiful dream and it is true, we both have to go, but you are indeed my Cinderella. Remember, I told you if the ring fits you are the one. And look at it, pulling her hand up for her to see the exquisite ring on her finger. Yes, you are the one, there is no doubt in my mind." He pulled her closer and kissed her. She melted like hot butter.

They quickly showered and vowed their love to each other. They checked out of the hotel and Dennis walked her to her car and they said their lengthy good-byes. Finally, Dennis concluded, "Don't forget to call me as soon as you get home Cinderella.

"I won't forget and thank you my Prince Charming", Leslie teased. "I will call you soon, she yelled as she drove off.

****

With no place to go, Michael returned to his room at the church and decided to speak to Pastor Sherman about his feelings and what transpired at Teresa's apartment. Momma King had just finished teaching and everyone was saying goodnight.

Perfect timing he thought; I will linger around and talk to Pastor Sherman. Perhaps he can help me make sense of the whole evening. He knew Pastor Sherman was a strong and sensitive man in the Spirit. He had great insight and compassion for mankind, especially those of the household of faith. He always went the extra mile in making sure their spiritual needs were met. He had a way to put you at ease and give great advice according to the Word of God. He took his calling to Shepherd God's people very seriously. He was always conscience that one day he would have to give an account to God for how he cared for them.

Michael was angry with himself and grateful to have Pastor Sherman to talk to. Michael decided he would be brutally honest with himself and tell everything that happened at Teresa's apartment. Perhaps Pastor could give some insight as to why he was rude to Troy. Why did he act territorial and jealous? Many thoughts ran through his mind that he did not understand. Why God would want to send me to the nations? I am still such a wicked and evil man. I thought I was born-again and was filled with God's Spirit. I should not act like this. What is wrong with me? As much as I hate to admit it; Teresa was right. I should have asked permission to buy those things for Jamie. And she was right to ask me to leave her apartment for being disrespectful to her friend Troy. Michael was distraught that Teresa was now angry with him and things did not go anything like he had hoped.

He shared a lot of information about his life including his past broken relationships he had with Teresa and Tavia. Pastor Sherman prayed inwardly asking God for wisdom to counsel his servant. He listened intently as Michael bared his

197

soul. At times, Michael would become very emotional. Pastor watched him very closely as the Holy Spirit began to unravel some of the hidden mysteries. At the appropriate time Pastor Sherman began to speak.

"Well, Michael let's take the matter to the Lord in prayer. *"Heavenly Father in the name of Jesus, I beseech you for the Wisdom of Counsel to rest upon me that I may be able to share your insight into this matter at hand. I ask that you will touch Brother Michael's heart to hear and receive your counsel with understanding, in Jesus' name. Amen."*

I admire your honesty and I know God is pleased because you did not try to hide your short comings and faults, but instead confessed them. In Proverbs the 28th chapter verse 13 says, *'That he who covers his sins shall not prosper but whoever confesses and forsakes them shall have mercy.'* See, *Brother Michael, by confessing your flaws, and not trying to hide them, the Word of God says you will prosper. What you are dealing with is your carnal nature. You will find in the book of Romans, the 8th chapter, verse 7, that the mind governed by the flesh is hostile to God, it does not submit to God's law. The carnal nature is what we constantly struggle with as a born-again Christian because we were born into sin and shaped in iniquity. That's why it is extremely important that we get our mind renewed – which is part of the sanctification process.*

"Huh? Help me. I don't understand what you are saying. How do you renew your mind and what is sanctification?" Michael asked.

"Well, the mind is renewed as you read, study and understand the Word of God. It changes the way you think. Knowledge empowers you. The more you read and meditate on the scriptures the more God opens up your understanding to His ways and what is acceptable and what pleases him. Once you begin to know the ways of God, you will begin to willingly forsake everything that is contrary to what God wants of you. That is the sanctification part. You set yourself apart from worldly and carnal things for God to use you for His Glory. God tells us to be holy for he is holy. Whenever we divert, we allow the enemy of God to keep us bound to doing the things we used to do that were carnal. This requires discipline and a made up mind to yield your body, soul and mind to the Spirit of God. You will not be able to do this victoriously without the Holy Spirit renewing your mind. Jesus is the keeper of your soul. That is why you felt jealous of the other guy that came to see Teresa. Even though you have not been in her life for the past nine years, you felt as if she was still yours and wanted to control some things in her life. The same with Jamie, you splurged on him, because of your absence in his life and you felt guilt. So you overcompensated for it. You have already received their forgiveness and God has forgiven you as well, right?"

Michael nodded his head wiping away the tears.

"Okay, now you have to forgive yourself. Do you understand?"

"Yes, Pastor Sherman. I do understand better now. I guess that is why God filled me with the Holy Spirit last week. I spoke in a language I never knew before and then he gave me the vision that I told you about earlier."

"Oh, yes, I remember very well. As you already know He is sending you to the nations. My assignment is to prepare you for what's ahead. I am glad we had this talk Brother Michael. God is preparing your heart to do awesome things for him and believe me, there is always purpose in the pain we experience as children of God."

"Pastor Sherman, I really appreciate your insight. I guess God has a lot of work to do in me; but I am determined to please God. The experiences I have had already have let me know that God is very real, powerful and loving. If he can turn me around and save me, as miserable as I was, then I know he really does love everyone because I was the most unlovable, Michael said, crying tears of joy."

Pastor Sherman smiled at Michael's humility and said, "Let's pray and give thanks."

CHAPTER 28

Judge Harris and Momma King were inseparable. He felt honored to drive her home from church every night. He attended every teaching on the Holy Spirit and could not believe how much he had grown spiritually. All the years he served as deacon in his church, it was very obvious that he was clearly missing something. He knew scriptures, he prayed and talked to God every day, but the joy and radiance that exuded from Pastor Sherman, Joni King and others seemed to be missing in his life.

"Les, thank you again for recording the teachings for me and driving me home, Momma King said, as she reached over and touched his hand. She suddenly sensed he was troubled by something. "Is everything okay Les?"

"Yes, Joni, believe me. It really was my pleasure to record your teachings and drive you home; but I keep wondering what is different about your relationship with God and my relationship with God? You seem to possess great wisdom, joy, love and a confidence in God like none other I've encountered. Plus you appear to have a sixth sense and know things that no one else knows. Just like now, you already seemed to know something was on my mind as if you could read it. What is it that you have that I am lacking?"

"Les, that is a very nice compliment and I am blessed that you can see God's love and gifts flow in me. Some of the gifts I taught on this week God have given to me. Since you asked, I think you are ready to know now. How about we discuss it when we get to my house over a cup of tea?"

"You think I am ready now for what?" He asked puzzled.

Momma King responded, "just wait until you get to my house. I just have to make a quick phone call to check on Teresa and Jamie."

"Why? Is something wrong with Teresa and Jamie?"

"No, but Michael was going over there tonight to have dinner with them and for the first time meet his son, Jamie. I just want to know how it turned out because just as I had finished teaching tonight, I saw him in the study talking to Pastor Sherman. I wonder if there was a conflict because her new friend, Troy Kennedy was supposed to stop there also tonight. I think she may have forgotten to cancel her meeting with Troy."

"Oh, I understand your concern. You are a kind, caring, wonderful mother image for Teresa and Jamie. They are blessed to have you Joni…and they are not the only ones blessed to have you, he said smiling. Momma King blushed.

They arrived at Momma King's house and she excused herself and rushed into her bedroom to make the call. Judge Harris had become very familiar with her kitchen and he busied himself making the tea and a light snack.

"Hello Teresa, It's me, Momma King. I was just calling to check on you and Jamie. How did the dinner go with Michael?"

"He may have changed in some ways, but he is the same jerk that he was when he left years ago. Tonight, he showed up with like nine years of toys for Jamie and no place to put them and when I complained, he suggested he get us a bigger apartment or a house. And to top that off, I forgot to call Troy and tell him we were not going to make it to church tonight and when he came, Michael verbally insulted him and I asked him to leave. He really infuriated me with his arrogance and smugness."

"Oh, sweetie, I am sorry that happened to you. How is Jamie doing?"

He is unscathed. Praise God. He is just excited about all of his 'new toys,' she said sarcastically.

"What kind of toys?"

"Oh, a Huffy two wheel bicycle, a fishing pole, skateboard, a pool table, a bible, lots of board games, a watch and a 50 gallon aquarium! Can you imagine all that in my apartment? He should have asked first, and I told him so!"

"Well, listen you can bring whatever doesn't fit to my house and he can play with them here when he comes here after school."

"Oh Momma King, that is a great idea. Thank you so much."

"No problem. Glad I can help. Now, tell me what happened that Michael verbally insulted Troy?"

Oh, Troy gave him a compliment about Jamie, telling him that Jamie was a really smart kid and how he was growing up into a fine young man; and Michael asked Troy with such a hostile attitude, "how would you know so much about my son?" Troy did not entertain his foolishness and left. I hope he isn't mad at me. He may not come back or call me again.

"Nawh, it will take more than that to stop a man from pursuing something he really wants, she chuckled. He'll be calling you again, trust me. Listen Sweetie, I gotta run now, but I have a Word of Knowledge concerning you.

"The Holy One of Israel says this week will be a trying week for you. You will be faced with several major decisions six months from now. You will question yourself if you are making the right decision, but don't fear He will guide you and

give you a solid confirmation. He will instruct you in the way which you shall go. My Peace will rest upon you when you have been justified."

"Well sweetie, I am here if you need me. Just know that God loves you so much that He took the time to forewarn you."

"Thanks so much for the prayer and the prophetic word. I will be watching Momma King."

"Well I gotta run now, Les is waiting for me."

"Okay, but who is Les?"

"Oh yes, I came over to tell you this morning but I forgot and I can't tell you now because he is here," she said whispering. "Momma King, you have a boyfriend?" Teresa asked in disbelief.

Momma King giggled and said, "No, I have a 'man friend.' I will tell you all about it tomorrow."

"Momma King I am so happy for you. I can't wait to meet him," Teresa shouted.

"Oh you did already."

"Huh? I did? Where at church?"

"No, I will tell you tomorrow. I have to run now. Give Jamie a hug for me. Bye."

Momma king hung up quickly to avoid answering more questions.

Teresa was feeling excited again after talking to Momma King. The prophetic word and Momma King's new relationship had diverted her attention away from Michael's narcissist behavior. "Oh my goodness," she beamed. "Momma King has a man. God does work in mysterious ways. Well, why not, she scolded herself...older people need love and companionship too," she concluded. Teresa finally got Jamie settled in bed and decided that she would read more of Ricky's letters tomorrow. She'd had enough drama for the day. She would take a nice hot shower and get things ready for work the next day. She could hardly wait to hear about Leslie's and Dennis' actually going out on a date.

CHAPTER 29

Judge Harris waited patiently for Joni. She came back in the room as he motioned her to the steaming hot tea he had made for her.

"Oh, you are spoiling me Les," she said giggling.

"I love spoiling you. In fact, I would like to take you for a weekend get-away. You have one more night to teach on the gifts of the Holy Spirit and I can hardly wait to get you alone with nothing to do but enjoy each other. What do you think?"

"Les, that sounds nice but I am not ready to make that commitment yet. I hope you understand."

Les pouted and sulked for a second and teased his way out of his bruised ego and rejection. "What? Am I losing my alluring appeal? If I was twenty-years younger I am pretty confident you would say yes."

"Your honor," she teased back. "I did not say no, I said I am not ready yet and if I was twenty years younger I would have said yes immediately."

After a good laugh and they settled down to sipping their tea, Les asked the question again, "Joni, what is it that you have that I am lacking spiritually?"

"Les, from all of our conversations and listening to the things you have shared with me, I believe you are lacking the Power of the Holy Spirit. Let me explain, Colossians 2:8 says, *'Beware lest any man spoil you through philosophy and vain deceit, after the tradition of men, after the rudiments of the world, and not after Christ.'*

"The Apostle Paul wrote this book of Colossians to warn the church and that implies us, because we are the church. He was saying to pay attention to men who will spoil you. They will tell you things that sound good, but it is really their own thought process or philosophy and vain deceit; and often times, they will share their own speculation and imagination instead of investigating their facts that they call truth. The idea is that the doctrines they taught were not sound doctrines to lead you to the truth, but instead, their doctrines were to lead one astray. This is still happening in so many of the churches today. They don't teach or preach on the Power of the Holy Spirit. This reminds me of Paul telling Timothy to study the Word for yourself to show yourself approved so you can rightly divide the Word of Truth. Paul goes on to warn us not to do things after the 'tradition of men,' meaning passing down traditions to the next generation, fostering the "rudiments of this world' and not after the Kingdom of God."

Les, I know this may sound like I am preaching, but I want to lay a foundation so you can really understand what may be lacking in your spiritual walk with God. *See, when you received salvation by asking Jesus Christ into your heart years ago, you conformed to the teaching of your church and never ventured out on your own to study about the gifts of God, but instead followed the traditions of old, and became religious, having a form of godliness, but unknowingly denied the Power of God; See Les, the next step was to be filled with the Power of God or another name, the Holy Spirit. He is a real person. He is the third person of the God Head. I believe what you are lacking is the baptism of God's Holy Spirit.*

"Joni, I think you are right. My church never talks about the gifts of God. I have only read about it. I can't believe I have been there all my life and did not know. I have learned so much since I met you. I did not understand many things but your teachings really enlightened me and filled me with hope. Now, my question is how to get filled with the Holy Spirit?"

Momma King was happy for him. He looked like a little boy and seemed to have unshakable faith. She quickly took advantage of the door that God had opened. She spoke with great compassion and authority as she explained her actions as she anointed him with the Holy Oil. He sat very still not knowing what to expect. Joni confirmed with him, so you want to be filled with the Holy Spirit right?

"Yes, he said, with his eyes squeezed tight and arms raised above his head.

"Well, Jesus said in the Gospel of Luke the 11th Chapter, verse 13, *'that if ye then, being evil, know how to give good gifts unto your children: how much more shall your heavenly Father give the Holy Spirit to them that ask him.'* She began to pray over him in tongues and suddenly said loudly in English, *'Les Harris receive ye the Holy Ghost in the name of Jesus Christ, the Son of the Living God!"*

Instantly he was speaking in a very distinct dialect. It sounded as if he was speaking Chinese. He leaped up from the table and began praising God as he spoke in the language God had given him. He was crying, laughing and dancing.

"I got Him now! He yelled. I got the Holy Spirit! Thank you Jesus! Thank you!"

Momma King joined in and they praised God for a long time.

"Thank you Joni, and thank you Jesus for filling me with your Spirit," he shouted. "It is almost midnight so I am going to let you get some rest but it is hard to come down from this high. I have never felt like this before." He kissed her on her forehead and gave her a very long hug.

Momma King blushed as her heart began to race. She dared not look up at him for fear he would kiss her on the mouth, so she kept her head down and said, "Good night Les, God is faithful."

"I feel like I could literally fly," he said, as he walked out the door.

"Well, please don't go jumping off buildings and force your Angels to have to catch you," she teased.

"Good night Joni."

CHAPTER 30

Teresa arrived early to work. She and Jamie both were excited to get back to their normal schedule. The vacation seemed to be just what the doctor ordered. She was elated to return to work and she was not the only one happy to have her back. Nate Bishop rushed over to greet her as she knocked lightly on his door and stuck her head in.

"Good Morning Nate," she smiled.

"Good morning Teresa, It is so nice to see you. Welcome back to Paradise," as he gave her a big hug. "Come on in and let me bring you up to date with the business." He was very pleased she seemed to be back to her old self. "Tell me, Teresa, tell me all about your vacation!" He asked excitedly.

Teresa shared her experiences on the vacation and that she and Jamie had a great time and she was now able to move on with her life. Ricky Clay was history and Troy's presence and their lengthy talks made her realize she was not only a beautiful woman but a woman that had a lot to offer and one that deserved respect.

Just as Teresa was leaving Nate's office she noticed Leslie at her work station. "Oh my goodness," Teresa exclaimed. "You look amazing this morning. You are glowing."

Leslie could not stop grinning. "Teresa you know I had almost given up. I had not been in a relationship for years and to meet Dennis, it is a dream come true. He is so handsome and just everything any girl could ever want."

"Oh wow," Teresa said, as she caught a glimpse of something shiny on her finger. She grabbed her hand staring at the huge solitaire diamond ring. What is this? Wait, I am confused now. This ring is from Dennis Hayes?"

"Yes," Leslie said. "Yes, it was love at first sight. We had an awesome weekend."

"I guess so," Teresa said, somewhat stunned. "I am really happy for you. I have never seen you so happy. He truly swept me off my feet and took me to meet his mother and convinced me that I was going to be his wife."

"Girl, you did more than that! Nate showed me the deal you made with him for the high end linen he purchased. You did an outstanding job! He paid full price! He always tried to negotiate the lowest possible bargain with me," Teresa scoffed.

Leslie reflected back. She had given him the price of the linen for all of his Bed and Breakfast Suites and he never tried to negotiate the price, he simply wrote out the check and gave it to me.

"Oh, really," Leslie chuckled. "Girl, I guess I did mess him up huh?"

"Yeah, girl he messed you up too! So tell me what happened and how did he come to ask you to marry him in forty-eight hours? Maybe I could learn a few things myself. I know I would have married Ricky in a heartbeat if he had asked. But I know now, that would have been the worst mistake of my life and I had been with him for almost three years."

"I know Teresa, I am so sorry. I thought you guys were the perfect couple. I longed to have what I saw with you and Ricky. How are you doing now?" Leslie asked.

"Well, Jamie and I went away for a week with my attorney to his country club."

"What?"

"You're dating again?"

"No, we are just friends. He is an older gentleman and not really my type, but he has some wonderful qualities about him that I really admire. He is very attentive to me and great with Jamie."

"I am glad you are moving on Teresa. You deserve to be happy. Don't rule him out because he is a little older. Just think of the experience he has to offer in *everything,*" she said wickedly.

Teresa smiled, remembering Momma King saying almost the same thing.

"Okay, enough about me. Tell me about you and Dennis Hayes."

"I probably should have waited before I gave myself to Dennis. I really regret that, but we both had way too much to drink and I think he felt bad for me and convinced me, he did not think any less of me...and in fact proposed to me. He kept telling me from the first time we met that I was going to be his wife. He even called me Cinderella and said, "If the ring he bought several years ago, fit my finger then he knew for sure I was the one. It fits perfectly and so did everything else, she said mischievously.

"Wow, that is crazy! It is like a fairytale story. It's too cute and almost unbelievable. But, I must tell you this. When I was sleeping with Ricky I thought it was okay because we were in love; but when I got saved and began to read His Word, God revealed to me that I was fornicating and sinning against Him and my own body. Yes, it was Roman's the 6th chapter. You and Dennis must read it, so you both will know," Teresa explained.

"Oh really? I didn't know that I was sinning against God and my own body. I guess I just never really thought about it. That's food for thought," Leslie confessed.

215

"Yeah it is a lot to think about. Tonight is Tuesday. It's the last night Momma King will be teaching on the nine gifts of the Holy Spirit at my church. She is an awesome woman of God. Remember she is the one who prayed for Nate Bishop and God instantly healed him."

"Oh yeah, I remember…that was a miracle! Wasn't she the same lady that warned you about Ricky too?"

"Yes, I am so sorry I did not take heed to her advice, but I am convinced that God knew I would not take her advice because I was so rebellious and immature that God had to allow my heart to be broken to get me to grow up. Growing up can be painful sometimes, but it is the pain that makes you see things from a different perspective. Anyway, why don't you come as my special guest tonight? I would love for you to meet my new friend as well as my ex… Jamie's father, Michael; He is back! Teresa said with a heavy sigh.

"Really, why did he come back after all these years?

"I don't know, but I think he is feeling guilty and now trying to over compensate for his absence with loads of gifts. He is studying to be a minister under the tutelage of my Pastor at Light of Love Ministries.

"What! Are you serious?" Leslie exclaimed.

216

"Yes," Teresa answered. "I think he is a work in progress. I can see in some ways he has changed, but he is still very self-absorbed and arrogant."

"Now wait a minute!" Leslie declared. "I remember my mother would always say, "A minister is a good catch if he is really sincere and loves God. If you marry a minister he will always treat you right because of his love for God and he would love his wife as Christ loved the church and as you already know, Christ died for His church."

"Well, now that is food for thought, but God will have to do a lot more work on this minister, Teresa mocked. So, getting back to the invitation, will you be able to come tonight?"

"I am not sure. Dennis is going to call me at nine tonight. I definitely don't want to miss his call. When does it start?"

"It starts at 7PM, it is usually about an hour long and you can have plenty of time to get home.

"Okay, great, I will see you there... at Light of Love on Prospect and Newfoundland right?" Leslie queried.

"Yes, Pastor Sherman's church. I am glad that you will be able to come; I think you will enjoy it." Teresa glanced down at her ring again. "Girl, that is some rock! It is absolutely gorgeous! I am really surprised because Dennis always seemed so business minded and focused. Had I known he was looking for someone I would have introduced you guys myself. I just assumed he had a woman as handsome as he is. He has one for sure now! Congratulations Leslie, I am very happy for you!

"Yes. And I think we better get to work before Nate fires us both," Teresa teased.

Leslie nodded giggling.

Later that afternoon, Teresa decided to call Troy's office to apology for Michael's insolence. He answered immediately.

"Troy Kennedy Law Firm, how may I assist you?"

"Hi Troy, It's Teresa. I just wanted to tell you I am sorry for Michael's actions towards you the other night."

"Well, it is okay. I just had no idea that he was there. Did he just show up and you did not have a chance to let me know he was going to be there for dinner? Teresa suddenly realized he had been hurt. "Yes, Troy you are right, he just showed up that morning and I was so taken back with him wanting to see Jamie, I hardly had time to do anything. And I totally forgot we had planned to go to church. Please accept my apology; I was just overwhelmed with his overbearing personality. He wanted to meet Jamie, so I thought it would be a good way to introduce him to his father over dinner. I tried to call you, but you were not in your office and I realized I did not have your home number and…"

"It's okay Teresa," he said interrupting her. I have no right to expect any explanation. But please take my home number now and make sure you use it," he said, trying to add a little humor to the situation. "Would you like me to pick you and Jamie up tonight?"

"Yes Troy, that will be great. Thanks for understanding. See you later."

"Okay, Talk to you in a bit," he replied and hung up. He was relieved to know that she really *did* care and did not deliberately stand him up. With that information, he decided he would not let her slip through his fingers. She is a keeper and he had to move quickly. He had worked all week trying to make her forget about Ricky and had great success, and now her ex is back. "I love a challenge," he said to himself.

CHAPTER 31

Dennis was so excited when he got home Sunday night, he could hardly wait to ask his mother, Gloria, if she liked her new daughter-in-law to be.   Gloria ran to the door to meet Dennis.

"Hey handsome, what are you up to?   I discern something is going on," she said knowingly.

"Yes Mom, I found my wife!! Did you like her?"

"I knew it! I knew it! She shouted. Oh, son, I am so happy for you…and yes, I loved her and she is beautiful. Did you tell your sisters yet?"

"No, Mom, I will tell them when I get back. Or you can tell them!" He shouted.

"When you get back? Where are you going?"

"I am going to check on all the suites on Monday to make sure everything is running well before I leave on Tuesday afternoon. I am planning to drive to New York to surprise her. I should be back sometime on Wednesday. I am hoping she will resign her job with Paradise Pillows and come and work with me…as my new partner and wife."

"Wow, Dennis I know you're serious, but have you given this a lot of thought? You just meet her right?"

Yes, Mom, but I know she is the one. I know it deep within my soul. She is the missing link in my life and I am sure of it! And guess what! Remember the ring I bought years ago and I told you this ring will confirm the person if it fits? And... It fits perfectly!!

"You already proposed and gave her the ring?"

"Yes, I did!"

"Well son, there is nothing left for me to say except I am happy for you, and I hope she makes you as happy as you are now. I guess I will be a grandma soon," smiling at the thought.

"Yes Mom, I am ready to be the best husband and father ever! I waited a long time for this. You really liked her?"

"Yes, son, I think she is a lovely girl and from our little short visit she seems to be very mature for her age. Yes, I liked her a lot."

"Okay Mom, I gotta get some rest. I must make sure all the suites are running well before I take off on Tuesday. Do you need anything tomorrow before I check on the suites?

"No son, I am fine. Thanks for asking."

"I love you to Mom. You are the best of the best and my favorite girl," he said, kissing her on her forehead. "Good night." Dennis walked out the door to his apartment in the basement.

"Good night son, I love you too."

Gloria was proud to have raised such a thoughtful, hardworking and very successful businessman. She could not have asked for a better son. Thinking about her two daughter's success in the medical field and her own life, she suddenly felt the overwhelming presence of God. She could not suppress the praise of thanksgiving that flowed from her lips. *"Thank you Lord Jesus. Oh God, when I think back to the days of living in the projects as a single mother, working two jobs to make sure every need was met; God you did it for us. You've brought us all from a mighty long way."*

****

Leslie rushed home from work to shower, grab a quick bite to eat before going to meet Teresa at church. She was nervous and excited. It had been a long time since she had gone to church. She had always heard a lot of good things about Light of Love church. She always promised herself that one day she would go and check it out. Well, this will be the day; after all so many great things have happened the last few days it would only be appropriate to go and give God his due benevolence, she thought. Leslie quickly dressed in her basic black dress with pumps and realized she should bring her Bible so she could follow along with the teacher.

"Dawg, Where is it?" she asked out loud.

She looked around her apartment for several minutes and finally found it. It had been tucked away in her bookcase along with the many books she had collected over the years. She dusted it off and hurried out the door. She had spent too much time looking for the Bible and now she was running a tad bit late. Just as she opened the door to leave, Dennis stood facing her. He was smiling his bright beautiful smile, but shocked at his presence, Leslie screamed.

"Dennis! What are you doing here?"

"I could not bear another day without seeing you. I thought I would surprise you."

"Well, that you did! But Dennis you really should have called. I am happy to see you but I am on my way out. I promised Teresa, you remember Teresa at Paradise Pillows right?"

"Yes, of course, I remember her."

"Well she invited me to church tonight and I promised her I would be there. Would you like to join me?"

"Sure, no problem. I will drive you. Can I kiss my bride to be first? He kissed her very passionately. Leslie pulled away. Dennis when church is over, we have to talk. I learned so much today about God and living a life that pleases him. I just want us to be on the same page."

"Wow, this sounds serious."

"It is. It is very serious and I just want us to be in a good place with God.

"Okay, Cinderella, let's get going," he teased.

"Okay, Prince Charming, she countered, hanging onto his arm.

CHAPTER 32

Wow, Teresa exclaimed holding onto Jamie's and Troy's hand. "The church is almost full and the service had not started yet. I can hardly wait to hear what Momma King has to say. This is your first time here right Troy?"

"Yes and I am looking forward to being refreshed. Thanks for inviting me," he said smiling tenderly at her. The Usher greeted them and escorted them to a few vacant pews near the front of the church.

"Teresa! Teresa! Wait up!" Teresa turned around to see Leslie and Dennis walking quickly to join them.

Oh, Leslie and Dennis, so nice to see you both. I didn't know you were coming Dennis..."

Leslie chimed in..."me either, but I am glad he is here." She said smiling.

"Congratulations! Dennis had I had known you were looking for a lovely lady; I would have introduced you to Leslie myself. I think you made an excellent and wise choice."

"Yes, I totally concur. She is my dream come true," he beamed.

"Awwwh, how sweet," both she and Leslie cooed.

"Oh, this is my friend and my attorney, Troy Kennedy and my son Jamie." Teresa said.

Dennis acknowledged both by shaking their hands, and took the seats the Usher had motioned him and Leslie to.

Soon everyone was seated and Teresa could feel someone staring at her. She turned her eyes in that direction of the "feeling" and saw Michael gazing at her with a look of disapproval. Teresa stared back, rolled her eyes and completely dismissed him. Just as she began to focus on what was happening in the front of the church, she noticed a man helping Momma King to the podium. As he turned back to take his seat Teresa could see his face clearly and her heart sank. "Oh my! It is Judge Les Harris! What on earth is he doing here? Why is he helping Momma King? What is going on?" she questioned. Teresa was suddenly stricken with fear. She grabbed Troy's arm. Troy looked at the fear etched on her face.

"Teresa, what's wrong?" he asked?

"It's Judge Harris. Look," she said startled, pointing in his direction. Just as Troy turned to see where she was pointing, Pastor Sherman walked over and shook Judge Harris hand before going to the pulpit to take his seat.

"It's okay Teresa, Pastor Sherman and Les Harris have been friends for years. Perhaps he invited him to hear Mother King teach. Remember this is our first night here and she has been teaching the past eight nights. Perhaps he has been here since the beginning and just decided to assist Mother King to the pulpit."

"No, it seemed like he knows her on a personal level. He was very friendly with her, she whispered and Michael is staring at us with daggers in his eyes.

"Teresa, I think you are reading too much into this. Let's just relax and enjoy the service Troy said trying to put her at ease. Please just ignore Michael, I am here and I will look after you and Jamie. Oh, wait a minute, Troy she whispered. "Did you say Les Harris?

Yes, Judge Les Harris.

"Why?" He questioned.

"Oh my goodness. I think he and Momma King are spending time together. That makes sense now. She mentioned her new friend name was Les and even told me that I knew him. Wow, look at God. I am very happy for her." Teresa smiled. "Troy they do look great together huh?"

"Yes, just like us," he whispered back.

The praise team took their position and suddenly there was a surrendered hush that fell in the place. They sang a few songs and the presence of God filled the temple and continued to linger when Mother King stepped to the podium to teach. She spoke with power and conviction defining each of the nine gifts that God has so graciously given to the body of Christ. *"I am going to recap on each of the gifts. The nine gifts are found in 1 Corinthians chapter 12 beginning at verse 8. God has given us these gifts through the Holy Spirit: The Word of Wisdom, The Word of Knowledge, Faith, The gifts of healing, the working of miracles, prophecy, discerning of spirits, divers (many) kinds of tongues, and the interpretation of tongues. The first one I want to define tonight is the **Word of Knowledge.** It is supernatural insight and knowledge specifically transmitted to you by the Holy Spirit on something that you would have no ability to know. The **Word of Wisdom** is the gift that gives you the ability to be able to properly apply knowledge to solve a problem or dilemma. The **Word of Knowledge** and the **Word of Wisdom** usually work together. The **Gift of Prophecy** is a specific and direct word from God to give to someone else. It is when God allows you to be an actual messenger on his behalf. The **Gift of Faith** is when the Holy Spirit manifests His own divine faith into you. It is a faith above the norm. It is the faith that produces supernatural miracles."*

There was such a hunger for the teaching. Many focused on writing every word Mother King spoke. She continued to define the **Gift of Healing**, the **Working of Miracles**, the **Discerning of Spirits**, **Divers Tongues** and finally the **Interpretation of Tongues**.

In her conclusion she reiterated that God wants to give us His gifts. *"God wants us to seek Him. He is the giver of the gifts. These gifts are not for you personally, but for the edification of the body of Christ."*

Teresa, Troy, Leslie and Dennis sat mesmerized. Even Jamie seemed to understand what was being taught. Teresa had totally lost focus of Judge Harris and her ex-boyfriend, Michael. She was now completely enamored with the teaching and desiring more of God.

Mother King finished her teaching early to ask those who desired an impartation of the gifts to come forth. Pastor Sherman met her as she came down from the podium and stood in front of the congregation. Many lined up in front of her and Pastor Sherman while the praise team sang. They laid hands on each person for the baptism of the Holy Spirit and an impartation of Spiritual gifts.

Troy, Teresa, Jamie, Leslie and Dennis all joined the line, eager to receive whatever God desired to give them. It seemed as if God was waiting on Leslie and Dennis. The minute Momma King laid hands on both of them and they both began to speak in tongues. They had no idea what had happen, but they were happy and unashamed, leaping and praising God. Troy, Teresa and Jamie were rejoicing and praising God as well. It was an awesome service!

When the service ended, Leslie and Dennis hugged Teresa and made their way to thank Momma King for praying for them. Just as they reached her, she smiled at them and said, *"I hear wedding bells ringing and you are getting married soon. God says to tell you both that His stamp and seal of approval is upon you and the union.* Overwhelmed with joy, they were suddenly leaping and praising God again. They experienced joy unspeakable. Leslie was so relieved at the words spoken by Momma King. She knew it was God letting her know it was His will for them to be married and Dennis was the long "waited for prize."

Michael made his way over to Teresa, Troy and Jamie. "Hi Teresa, It's nice to see you all again. I am glad for the opportunity to apologize to you and Troy. Please forgive me for my inappropriate comment to you the other night at Teresa's home. I was out of line and I am truly sorry I over stepped my boundaries. Troy nodded his head and said, "no problem Man." as they shook hands. Feeling a little uncomfortable, Michael turned and focused on Jamie.

"Hey Jamie, it is nice to see you again."

"Hi Mr. Michael," Jamie said politely. "I am glad you came to church. I love to go to church with Mama. I always feel so happy when I come."

"Yes Jamie. Me too! If it is okay with your Mama, maybe I can stop by soon and take you fishing."

"Yes! I know a good place to go. It is where Ricky used to take me fishing! Mama can I go fishing with Mr. Michael? Please?"

"Jamie, calm down. We will talk about this later. There are a few things I still have to talk to Mr. Michael about, glaring at him. I have to let him know that if he wants to take you anyplace to speak to me about it FIRST!"

"Uh oh, I did it again huh? I am sorry Teresa, really I am. Please forgive me. I am inexperienced with what is protocol. I am learning and I promise I will try my best not to annoy you. I will call you tomorrow if that is okay?"

Teresa did not answer but instead asked, "Michael will you please excuse us? Jamie, please say good night to Michael."

"Good night," as Troy led them towards the door. "Oh, wait, I gotta tell Momma King what a great job she did tonight," she said. They made their way over to Momma King, just as Judge Harris was helping her gather her things to leave. Judge Harris looked directly at Troy and Teresa... "Well, well, well, it is nice to see you both," he said smiling. Troy smiled and shook his hand.

"Yes, Teresa, this is my friend Les," Momma King said proudly.

"Hi Judge Harris... Yes, it is nice to see you in this type of setting," she said laughing. "This is my son Jamie."

"Hello Mr. Harris, "Jamie said politely.

"Oh, Joni, should I give this to Teresa now?" as he picked up the tape recorder.

"Yes, I gave Les the assignment to record all the teachings for you, so if it is not right, he is the one in trouble," she teased.

"Oh, that was nice of you. Thank you Judge Harris. I am sure he did an outstanding job," she said smiling, as she took the tape recorder.

He gave her a warm hug and said, "I hope we can be friends because I am crazy about your Momma King."

Mother King blushed and reached out to Jamie and gave him a big kiss.

"Absolutely the best friend ever, she replied laughing as she looked at Troy. "It is to my advantage to be the best friend I can be right Troy?"

They all laughed. "Yes, it is always good to be friends with the Judge, Troy replied.

"Momma King, I am happy for you," Teresa said beaming.

"And I am happy for you and Troy too."

"Oh, we are just friends Teresa said defensively…

"Yeah, yeah, yeah…and we are just friends too," Momma King snapped back smiling.

CHAPTER 33

Michael was feeling sad as he went to his guest quarters. He did not mean to upset Teresa again. He felt badly that he was misunderstood. He did not mean to ask Jamie to go fishing before speaking to Teresa first, it just happened. It was not deliberate. Michael knelt down beside his bed and cried out to God. *"Please help me to be more considerate of others, especially Teresa and Jamie. I want to win them back. Please let them know I really do love them both. And Father help me to retain the teachings of the Holy Spirit that Momma King taught this week. Continue to bless her and give her divine wisdom to teach."*

Just as he was getting up, he noticed a letter on the floor. It appeared to have been pushed through the crack under the door. He did not notice it there when he came in. Or did someone just leave it while I was praying, he thought. Well either way, let's see who is writing to me as he picked up the letter.

Michael had written State Trooper Auggie and Charlie shortly after he arrived in New York as he promised. He often thought of Trooper Auggie and his powerful testimony and wondered if he and his wife reconciled.

No, it wasn't Trooper Auggie writing back, it was a letter from Charlie. Michael's mood quickly changed. He was so happy to hear back from him so quickly. He was excited as he ripped the letter open. Inside the letter was another smaller envelope that said, do not open until last.

Dear Michael,

I was overwhelmed with joy to hear from you. I miss you very much and I just wanted you to know that you literally changed my life forever. God sent you to me and I did not realize exactly why until after you left. It was the monetary gift you gave me that was a supernatural blessing. I was able to fix up my house a bit and buy some new furniture and three new suits for church! For years I felt ostracized because of my appearance and often cried to God because I was so ugly. I felt so lonely and undesirable. It was through you that the blessing came and God answered my prayers. Please open the smaller envelop now.

Love, Charlie.

P.S. Pastor Jo sends his love, prayers and many thanks for your generosity towards him as well. I am attending church in town with him now.

Michael quickly opened the smaller envelope and a picture of Charlie fell out. Michael stood in shock with his mouth wide opened. He barely recognized him. The back of the picture stated: "After the plastic surgery with my potential wife!" "Oh my God, it was a miracle!" Charlie was smiling with a full set of teeth, the wart had been removed from his nose, his hair was still pumpkin orange but was cut closely to his head. He was clean, shaven and well dressed in a dark brown suit. He looked amazingly handsome. "Unbelievable"!! Michael was filled with compassion as he wept and gave thanks for his friend's transformation. "To God be the Glory," he shouted.

****

Troy took Jamie and Teresa home after church. They had a light casual conversation during the ten minute drive. Teresa thanked Troy as they approached her apartment. Jamie seemed more quiet than usual. Just as he was to get out of the car, he thanked Troy and said Goodnight."

"Goodnight Jamie," he replied.

"Mama, I had such a good time in church and it is getting late, can I skip my shower tonight. I want to take the time to pray and read my Bible. So can I skip my shower just for tonight?"

Puzzled by his willingness to pray and read his Bible, Teresa asked "are you feeling okay?"

"Yes, Mama I feel real good. I feel God gave me a special gift tonight Mama. I don't know what it is, but He gave me a gift," he said without wavering. "And Mama, you don't have to come in now if you don't want to, I can let myself in with my key."

Troy smiled, "you have really become a responsible young man and you trust me with your mama?" Troy teased.

Jamie said, "yes, that's right Troy. I know you are a nice man and you would never hurt my Mama."

Teresa beamed proudly and said "okay Jamie, but I will be there in a minute. Wow, Troy, he really is growing up fast. I love how his heart has turned towards the things of God at such a young and tender age. I just hope God gives me wisdom to raise him in the right way."

"Oh without a doubt," Troy said. "You are an excellent mother. Jamie is very fortunate to have you as his mother. I am equally fortunate to have you as my friend." Teresa smiled and said, "Thank you Troy, but *you* are really the 'good friend'. And speaking of friends, could you give me some friendly advice. Off the books of course?"

He laughed. "Sure how can I help?"

"It's Michael, Jamie's father. I think he means well but he is trying too hard to make up for his absent years in Jamie's

237

life and he is constantly overstepping his boundaries with me. How can I get him to understand that he must speak to me first about any role he wants to play in Jamie's life? Do you think I am being unreasonable?"

"No, not at all Teresa. I think you handled him very nicely this evening at church. Although, I think you are right. I think he means well too, but he can't just do whatever he wants with Jamie without your consent. If you would like I can provide you with legal documentations for him with certain and specific instructions."

" No, I hope it doesn't get that far, but I appreciate your offer. He will probably come by tomorrow after I get off from work to see Jamie. I will reiterate my expectations."

"Thank you, Troy for being here. I guess I will get in and check on Jamie."

"Okay Teresa," as he reached over and took her hand in his. Teresa turned and gazed into his eyes. He leaned over and kissed her on her forehead. Troy knew she desired him to kiss her, but he held back to make sure she would not regret anything, and when he did… she would be hungry for his kiss and want more.

She said, "Good night Troy."

"Good night Teresa, may I call you tomorrow?"

"Sure," she said and never looked back. She was actually annoyed that he kissed her on her forehead again. She suddenly realized she had mixed emotions. A part of her wanted to be only friends, but the other part wanted a more personal and intimate relationship. *"Father please help me to get this flesh under subjection to your Spirit. He has aroused the "old fornicating Teresa." Help me Lord Jesus."*

Jamie had finished praying when Teresa came into the house. She peeked in his room as he was getting in bed with his Bible. She did not want to disturb him. She decided to take her shower early and get ready for bed. The hot shower was refreshing and energizing. So many things ran through her mind. Michael, Troy, Judge Harris and Momma King, the gifts of the Holy Spirit, Leslie's and Dennis's engagement and then there was Ricky Clay and the growing numbers of his unread letters. After showering she peeked into Jamie's room, he was fast asleep holding his Bible to his chest. He looked so peaceful. Teresa kissed him and turned off the light.

CHAPTER 34

Over the next several months, Michael worked extremely hard not to annoy Teresa. Jamie began to warm up to him and soon began calling him "DaddyMike." Teresa felt relieved and happy for Jamie; he had two strong men in his life who deposited positive things in his life. He did not mention Ricky's name much and when he wasn't doing things with Michael, he was going on ventures with Troy. It was a huge surprise to Teresa when Jamie announced that he was going fishing with Troy and Michael. The weekends were full of adventure and fun for Jamie. He grew very fond of them both. During the week, after supper, he spent most of his time in his room reading and praying. Things were going very nicely until several of the nine gifts of the Holy Spirit began operating in Jamie's life.

Teresa had just settled down to read a few more of Ricky's letters when Jamie came bursting through the bedroom door.

"Mama! Mama! God is training me to preach his Word and I will travel the world telling of the goodness of Jesus. He told me miracles will follow my ministry and my hands are holy. He told me that you will be getting married six months from this date and Ricky is coming back home!"

"Whoa, Whoa, Jamie! What are you talking about?" She asked puzzled.

"Mama, it is true! God told me when I was praying tonight. I was just talking to Him and when I became really quiet I heard him say those things to me. Mama, please believe me! Ricky is coming home. Aren't you happy?" he questioned.

"Yeah sure Jamie, why don't you go back to bed now and we will see how you are feeling in the morning," she said, still dazed at the news. *"Oh, God, Is this really true?"* She thought as she crawled back into her bed. Unable to sleep, Teresa sat Indian style in her bed and decided to read the rest of Ricky's letters. Only seven more letters lay unopened and it was then that she noticed she had not received a letter from him in over a month. She quickly opened the next letter in its chronological order. It was the same as most of his letters in the past, repeating how much he loved her and Jamie and saying how sorry he was for letting them down. He mentioned how he was growing in his walk with God and teaching his fellow inmates the Bible. His charismatic personality won over again even in prison. He was well liked and respected as a positive leader in prison. He always mentioned that her name had been approved so she could correspond and visit him; still he confessed his love and longed to see her and Jamie.

Finally the next to the last letter was very brief but filled with lots of hope.

My Dearest Teresa,

I hope you and Jamie are doing well. I miss you both so much. I was just informed that the President of the United States is considering clemency for non violent offenders like myself, who have been incarcerated for drug trafficking. I qualified because you did not press charges on me for kidnapping. Thank you again. I owe you so much and I am going to make it all up to you and Jamie.

I applied for executive clemency and I was advised that the Presidential Commutation has been granted. I know it will still be a while before I am actually released due to the paperwork involved. I will write you as soon as I know. I am looking forward to seeing you and Jamie again. I am rejoicing and praising God for another opportunity to be the best Christian I can be with you by my side. I love you Teresa,

Ricky

Teresa could hardly breathe. *Oh my God, it's true. Jamie said "You had given him a gift after Momma King taught and prayed for an impartation to the people. Oh my God, Ricky is really coming home! Oh Wait! Jamie said I would be married within 6 months from today...Can that too be true?"* Teresa grabbed the last letter. She was shaking so badly she was having difficulty opening it. Finally opened, she snatched the contents of the letter out and began to read:

My Dearest Teresa,

"Yes, my dear, it is true. I will not be able to write anymore after this letter, but I will be home Saturday, May 19th."

Oh my Goodness! She screamed, glancing at the calendar. That is this weekend! She cried uncontrollable of tears. She looked at the postmark on the letter and it was dated March 10th. It has been over a month since he had written her. Teresa thanked God for allowing her to read the letters now at such an appropriate time. She was also happy that Jamie and Michael were going camping Friday after school to do some father-son bonding. They planned to be back early Sunday morning to go to church. Troy had to go to Albany on business and would return on Monday. She praised God that she would be able to talk to Ricky alone when he came on Saturday.

Glancing back at the letter, Ricky continued:

"Teresa, I know this may be a lot to ask, but I hope you will allow me to stay with you and Jamie until I can get on my feet again. We can finally be the family you always wanted us to be. I don't have a lot of personal belongings, so I won't take up too much space. I look forward to seeing you and Jamie real soon.

I love you,

Ricky

"What! And he wants to come here to stay? *Oh, God what am I going to do. This is too much I need your help Jesus.*" Teresa folded the letters and put them back in the envelope. She sat stunned in her bed overwhelmed with joy, fear, and a myriad of emotions. She kept going over in her mind the prophetic word that Jamie spoke, and Ricky really is coming home and she was going to be married in six months. Not only was he coming home, but he wants to stay with us. **Once more on the edge**, she cried herself to sleep wondering, "how did I get into this situation? What will Momma King think? What will Troy do? What is Michael going to say? How is all of this going to affect Jamie?"

CHAPTER 35

Meanwhile, Troy arrived in Albany late Friday afternoon. The first seminar will start at 7PM that evening. He ordered a light dinner in his room and found himself day dreaming again. He made it to the evening seminar but could not concentrate. The lecturer was explaining the new laws that had recently passed and Troy could not stop thinking of Teresa. He was convinced that she cared for him more than she let on. "One thing for sure, I will find out when I get back. I am going to make her and offer and hopefully she will not refuse. If she does refuse, I will move on. I will try to continue to have a relationship with Jamie; if she is okay with that, but I will not waste anymore time trying to win Teresa's love. I am convinced now that she is clearly not interested in Michael but if it was Ricky that could be another story. She really loved him. It has been almost a year since her ordeal with Ricky Clay. Ricky really broke her heart and she was devastated. I have shown her a lot of affection and great friendship hoping to win her love and help her to heal; I never crossed the boundaries she set with me as her friend. Even when I know she wanted me to kiss her. I remained true to her as a friend, even though it was pretty hard on a brother; he winced with pain as he thought of how his masculinity was stirred.

"Yes that's exactly what I will do when I get back," he declared. "I will go to the jeweler's and get her a beautiful ring, and ask her to be my wife."

After a long sleepless night, Troy decided it was senseless to stay for the weekend seminar. Teresa and Jamie had captured his thoughts to the point he could not focus on anything but them. Troy checked out of the hotel early Saturday morning heading back home, convinced that Teresa loved him. His love for her was not a question. Today is the day. He drove straight to JD Jewelers' arriving just as they were opening.

"Hello, Mr. Kennedy," JD said smiling as he opened the door.

"What can I do for you this fine morning?"

"Hi JD, It's nice to see you. I want a diamond engagement ring that is really special and unique. JD, the polished and experienced salesman that he was, never offered his best until last. He decided to hold back the one of a kind diamond wedding ring that was just shipped in from Dubai last week. JD was confident it will be the one he would want. He showed Troy several rings from the showcase, but nothing seemed to hold his interest. JD thought to himself; okay now is the time. "Oh, Excuse me Mr. Kennedy, I have something in the back I would like to show you. Please make yourself comfortable and I will be right back."

"Sure," Troy said.

JD came back smiling with a gold box. Inside the gold box was a black suede ring box. He carefully opened it and the moment Troy saw it ... he said, "Yes, that's it!" It was a gorgeous platinum five carat diamond ring in the shape of an Octagon. The engagement ring sat elegantly inside the wedding band which surrounded the huge octagon in purple and pink diamonds. It was like none other. "Yes, Troy said...this is it!"

"Should I wrap it for you Mr. Kennedy."

"No, that will not be necessary; I will take the black suede box only. I don't want to fumble trying to open boxes. I am already nervous, he laughed.

Well, I am sure you will get a yes when she sees this beauty! Is it someone here in the community?

"Yes, but I will let you know who she is when she says yes." Troy thought, "now why does he need to know that?"

JD smiled sheepishly as he took Troy's credit card.

Troy took the box and headed for the door. "Thanks JD and if she says yes, I will make sure you are invited to the wedding."

JD smiled. "Well good luck Mr. Kennedy, thanks for your business."

CHAPTER 36

Jamie and Michael made great progress in their relationship. Their camping trip that weekend removed all barriers. They laughed, and prayed together, they shared their fears, their faith in God, their goals and their trust and confidence in God. Jamie shared with DaddyMike the influence Momma King had on him and the Bible stories she told him. He shared that she would pray in an unknown tongue and anoint him with oil and it made him feel warm and tingly inside. They sat and talked for hours around the campfire.

"Oh and DaddyMike, the other night when I was praying, God gave me some gifts," he said excitedly.

"Really how do you know?" Michael asked.

"Well He told me I would travel all over the world preaching and my hands were anointed and He will use me to perform miracles."

"Wow, that is awesome!"

"Yep," and he told me that Mama is getting married in six months." Jamie did not tell DaddyMike that God told him that Ricky was coming home also. He noticed DaddyMike seemed to be uncomfortable when he mentioned Ricky's name.

"Really Jamie? Did God tell you who your Momma is going to marry?"

"No Sir, but I saw her walking down the aisle at Pastor Sherman's church. She was dressed in a long wedding gown and she was so beautiful and happy."

"Well Jamie, God told me he was sending me to the nations and maybe when you finish school you could come help me preach. Wouldn't that be nice if your momma could come with us?"

"Yes, DaddyMike, that would be very nice in the natural, but it's best if we do what God's spirit wants us to do. I remember reading Jeremiah 29:11 that God has the plan for our lives and it is a good plan if we do what He wants us to do.

"Wow, Jamie, you are one wise young man! I know God has given you insight beyond your years. I am very proud of you and the man you are becoming. Come here Jamie. I want to bless you. Jamie kneeled in front of him and Michael laid his hand upon his son's head as he looked out into the universe of the many stars that hovered above and said: "First Jamie, I ask you to please forgive me for abandoning you when you were first born."

Jamie said, "it's okay DaddyMike, you are here now and that is what really matters. I forgive you."

Again, Michael was almost lost for words at his son's level of maturity. He knew God had something really special for his life.

"Thank you Jamie, now I want to bless you. This is something I should have done when you were first born. I am so grateful and honored to be able to do it now. *Dear Father, the Creator of this beautiful universe, I stand before You to bless my son. I dedicate him back to You for Your perfect will to be done is his life. May the Lord bless you my son, Jamie Hayward and keep you. May the Lord make His face to shine upon you, and be gracious to you. May the Lord lift up His countenance upon you and give you peace. May you walk in power, prosperity and humility and always in obedience to the Word of God. May He fulfill the plan, the thought and the purpose He has for your life in Jesus' name. Amen.*"

They both cried and held each other. It was a very special moment for the both of them. Michael could not help but think; perhaps Teresa will marry him after all and they can be the perfect family. Smiling at that thought, he said, "okay buddy, it's time for bed as they crawled into the camping tent."

CHAPTER 37

Jamie and Michael were not the only ones who made giant steps in their relationship over the weekend.

Leslie and Dennis eloped and got married in Jamaica. Leslie resigned from Paradise Pillows to help Dennis manage his Bed and Breakfast suites in New Jersey. She and Dennis are looking forward to starting their family and Gloria is ecstatic at the idea of becoming a grandma.

Momma King and Judge Les Harris became inseparable. They love each others' company and spend every free moment together.

Michael received a letter from Trooper Auggie. He and his wife were remarried and they had just returned home from a Caribbean cruise where they became reacquainted as husband and wife.

Troy arrived at Teresa's around 10:30AM. He sat in the car looking at the ring trying to build up enough courage to propose to her. He prayed for strength and God's will to be done. Finally at 11:00AM, Troy knocked on Teresa's door. Teresa raced to the door because she thought it was Ricky. Stunned and obviously confused, she said "Troy, what are you doing here? I thought you were in Albany."

"I was, but may I come in?"

"Sure," as she stepped aside and followed him into the apartment, leaving the door slightly ajar.

"Well, I am sorry for just barging in on you without calling but I couldn't concentrate in Albany during the Seminar, so I left this morning and came here. I have something to tell you. Teresa, I love you and have been in love with you since last year when I represented you. I know we have agreed to be friends, but I can no longer pretend to be just your friend. I am a man that loves you and Jamie deeply, but if this is not what you want, I will respect that and I will never ask you this question again."

He paused and kneeled before her with his back to the door; he pulled the box from his Sports Jacket and displayed the ring...It looked amazingly beautiful and rich.

"Teresa will you marry me?"

Teresa stared speechless at Troy and the ring he was holding, when suddenly she was distracted by the door opening.

"Ricky!" She screamed but could not move.

Troy stood up and turned to face the intruder. Shocked to see Ricky Clay, Troy said, "Should I call the police to report an escaped prisoner?"

Ricky smiled smugly, "well, well, well, look like I got here just in time!"

Troy and Teresa ignored his sarcasm.

Teresa finally said, "no, he received clemency and he is out for good."

"Oh, and you knew he was coming huh?" Not waiting for a reply from Teresa. Troy said, "Okay, well I guess you both have a lot of catching up to do." He turned and walked out the door, still holding the ring in his hand. He suppressed the tears that were inevitable because of the pain in his heart until he reached his car. He was devastated and distraught. The tears came strong and forceful, they would not stop flowing. He cried out to God, "Why? God Why?" as he drove home.

Ricky walked over to Teresa who was still in shock. He gave her a big hug. She hugged him back but still could not speak.

"Hey, where's Jamie?" He asked looking around.

"Teresa! Teresa! Where is Jamie?"

"He... he... went camping," she finally stuttered.

"Oh, okay. When is he coming back?"

"Sunday."

"Great that gives us a little time alone and time to get caught up on the past year. I am a little hungry and I used my last five dollars to come here. Do you have anything cooked or could we go to Lil Lady Elite and get a bite to eat?"

"Yes, sure" Teresa said, "Let me get my purse, I will be right out." Teresa went into her bedroom, closing the door. She kneeled quickly and cried out… *"God, please tell me how to handle this situation, in Jesus name."* As soon as she stood up, she knew exactly what to do. She smiled at God and said, "thank you Jesus. Thank you!"

Ricky talked non-stop, professing his love and how things will be now that he is back… blah, blah, blah. He was still talking nonstop when Teresa stopped at the bank. "Ricky I will be back in a few minutes." Okay, no problem he said, turning up the radio as Roberta Flack sang, "Killing me softly."

"Yes, that is appropriate," Teresa thought as she closed the car door. Teresa returned after a while and drove Ricky to Lil Lady Elite. Ricky continued to talk all the way there. As they parked at their once upon a time favorite restaurant, Ricky got out of the car to open the door for Teresa. She did not budge. She spoke to him through her window. Ricky, I brought you here so you can get yourself something to eat. I am not hungry. She reached into her purse and said, "In this envelope is the $10,000 you gave me and Jamie. It should be enough to get you a place to stay, and also enough to leave the area and get a

254

fresh start someplace, but not here. Please leave me and Jamie alone. It has been a little over a year now and Jamie and I have come a long way trying to heal emotionally from all that you put us through. I can not allow the old wounds to resurface. I forgive you. God bless you and Goodbye Ricky. Teresa drove off leaving him speechless with his mouth open holding the envelope.

Teresa drove unswervingly to Troy Kennedy's condominium. She parked her car and raced to his door, ringing the bell. Troy was reluctant to open the door because his eyes were swollen and red and he did not want to see or talk to anyone. The bell rang again. Frustrated and annoyed, he snatched opened the door. "Teresa? What are you doing here?"

I came to say "Yes, you didn't wait for my answer. Yes, Troy Kennedy. I will marry you!" Troy began crying again, but this time, they both cried tears of joy.

SIX MONTHS LATER TO THE DATE OF JAMIE'S PROPHECY...Teresa Hayward's quest for love and happiness had been sanctioned by God the Father and she married the man that God had for her... Congratulations Mrs. Troy Kennedy!

Dear Reader:

Thank you so much for your love and support. I hope you enjoyed the book.

If you would like to contact me please visit my website, www.planthoughtpurpose.com or my email account which is crobinson420@yahoo.com.

Continued blessings and many thanks…

Carrie E. Robinson